A Concussed History of Scotland

A Bad Day for the Sung Dynasty (1984)

The Intelligent Observation of Naked Women (1987)

Ridiculous! Absurd! Disgusting! (1989)

A Very Quiet Street (1989)

A Concussed History
of Scotland

Frank Kuppner

Polygon
EDINBURGH

© Frank Kuppner 1990

Polygon
22 George Square, Edinburgh

Set in Linotron Sabon
by Koinonia, Bury and
printed and bound in Great Britain by
Redwood Press Limited
Melksham, Wiltshire

British Library Cataloguing in
    Publication Data
Kuppner, Frank, *1951–*
    A concussed history of Scotland.
    I. Title
    823'.914

ISBN 0 7486 6059 3

When someone asked him if he had no
care for his country, he replied:
'Be quiet — I have the greatest
care for my country', pointing to
the heavens.

> *Lives of the Philosophers*
> Diogenes Laertius
> [Anaxagoras]

Chapter 1

Go away – I wish to have nothing to do with you. I insist on
it. Go away! After all, I am in a position to be able to insist. I
intend simply to wait here quietly until my equal (whom you
might call the entire universe) comes along. After all, the only
sure way of escaping the torments of an emotional disaster, is
to find another one.

And, indeed, how could you possibly not go away, given
that nothing except me exists anyway? As for the Universe –
the Universe is merely something which I created as an
illustration of my own non-existence. Call it a metaphor, if you
like.

Chapter 2

After all, if childhood is a tomato on a chair, old age is merely
the chair. The tomato is now on the table. The eyes of a
lecherous (or venomous) old lady are the eyes of a girl who
cannot get out of bed. The eyes of a girl, on the other hand, are
the eyes of a girl. For only females can truly be said to have eyes
– that is something else which you will probably never manage
to find out for yourselves. Now, bearing all that in mind, tell
me: what is that, whirling around in the air like a wall that has
stood for too long? Is it age? Is it youth? Is it me? Is it – I am
forced by my neighbours to ask – neither? In the end, you all
fall out of people's heads, and out of your own heads fall the
clothes which you leave in untidy heaps on so many tidy floors.
This, you think, should be enough to save you, but it won't
save you. Always you leave behind a cramped, less comfortable position, to find yourselves in a more cramped, less
comfortable position.

Chapter 3

Or am I the only one who has noticed the million and more different varieties of sleeping? Am I the only one who has noticed how often you are beset by sharp momentary stabbing pains – I mean actual physical phenomena – reality, reality (remember that?) – which would be intolerable if they lasted any longer than they do, but which, lasting as briefly as they do, you never mention even once during your lives? No? Look at the hands of sleeping women. Did the movements of those small objects create all of this, and all of me with it? I think at times that my only regret is that the women I have loved have so often done the wrong things with their perfect priceless mouths. This is 80% a reference to speech. It is only 17% unmitigated filth. Up and down the waves beat against the old wall. This is almost exactly what they will continue to do when the wall has disappeared. Darkness covers all; much as light would do. Hello? Are you there? No? I thought not.

Chapter 4

Why, then, am I sitting here in this tawdry Japanese hut, exposed to the wind and the rain? Is there no-one here who will answer me? All I am waiting for, basically, is someone to talk to.

Chapter 5

Am I, merely because nothing exists, or nothing yet exists, to be denied companionship? I long to hear the curve of an answering spiral – an equal infinity to add to my own and thereby make life possible. I am equal to you only in that I do not know who I am. In all other respects, I am far superior. For instance, I have moved beyond your own absurd (even if correct) notions of past, present and future.

Chapter 6

However, by all means continue to eat an egg roll with elegance sufficient to fill a street – and a far longer street than this one, I or my dead twin might add! – while I continue to wrestle unsuccessfully with problems of formulation. When I see you drinking water, it seems to me that I am seeing something more important than the creation of a world of liquid. Adorable ambiguity! When I see you drinking alcoholic beverages, I think: as soon affect a million sunsets as the composition of her brain. I do not know if every woman's small mouth is big enough to hold the whole of history. She opens the door and comes through from the next room. That is the sort of thing that women do. Let us not exaggerate its importance merely because it smashes out a window into our brain, through which an intolerably beautiful scent drifts, which causes us to sneeze repeatedly from sheer joy. Or from some other terminal disease. Ah! We are in the same room! And we are still in the same room! How is this possible? Oh, look! It is turning red, and swelling out to 50 times its normal size! Who would have expected that?

Chapter 7

Actually, I do not know what to expect. Which is to say, I expect nothing. Which is to say, I am obviously not alive. Or can there be life without expectation? Perhaps it is possible.

Oh, I do not deny that the news that the world had almost ended during the night caused me a certain amount of heart-searching. For a few moments, I deliberately refrained from listening to music. Sometimes the door of a house opened, and a face glanced out for a moment or two, before retiring, shocked. The young were behind an occasional street-wall – perhaps every fifth or so. I no longer remember. It is not important. I telephoned her yesterday, and she advised me to go away. I opened a door and went through it, as did so many other people. Who is that floating above the ground over there anyway? And thus definitively ended a sad period of my life. Or what would have been a sad period of my life had I actually been alive.

Chapter 8

Or so I thought at the time. I feel a terrible tiredness come over me, like a leg descending from the sky, as if an omen. Let me look out of this window. Is it a window? Can I be sure?

Chapter 9

After all – today for the first time I looked in a mirror and saw myself as old.

Actually, the truly surprising thing was to discover that I was a sort of dog.

Children were running by on the road outside, presumably to school, as usual.

Their parents, as usual, were widely spread throughout the city.

Chapter 10

Parents? Do parents exist? The idea that someone with a complicated brain is merely a preparation for another complicated brain is an untenable argument for anyone with a brain like your own. You will notice that I resisted the temptation to talk of your soul's rectum, or even to marvel at how it creeps along the wall, like encroaching sunlight. The child sleeps. The mother sleeps. Are they three people? Was it yesterday or the day after when I last looked at them? It seems that they were thrown onto the shore by the first wave. You must know that there is a distant shore in the universe – you must penetrate Coma Berenices to reach it – a haphazard scatter of stars – if you are fortunate she will let you observe her hair some rainy afternoon in front of a flickering television set on which people lugubriously sing. After all, is a man to be called a pervert merely because he keeps a box of not hairless armpits beneath his bed? One cannot live entirely without friends. In the long hours of the night, when one appears to be awake, having slipped unnoticed through the secret entrance, what else is one to do? Am I to spend my whole life in the wrong room?

Chapter 11

Yet in fact a few thousand at times violent at times motionless oceans have raged or have calmly extended themselves over this surface, before ever they lay here together on a bed. And who occupied this house before us? There was a child then too, who was always at various stages of youngness. You creep along the contiguous wall, reach a corner, begin to creep along the contiguous wall. I have continued to creep round these walls for what seems like an infinite number of mornings, and usually I recognise the people whom I see. Oh, there are of course occasional inexplicable change-overs. Oh, look, the baby is beginning to talk! Oh, look! Another one beginning to talk. And so they all talk, shout, whisper to each other, scream, then go away and are soon replaced. But the sunlight I recognise, although it does not charm me now as once it did five times ten to the nine years ago, (5,000,031,000), when the future seemed promising. Yet, if I did have a wife, I would adore her, particularly her complicated antennae. Do you think she is ignorant of that? Please come closer to me, that I might fail to touch you in a more involving manner.

Chapter 12

It is a pleasant, almost overwhelmingly erotic afternoon. There is intermittent activity in the roads outside – and that is not merely a reference to the branches of the trees waving languidly in the air, as if seeking to persuade young women that they too could reveal subtle cleavage if they really wanted to, or ride bicycles down a street almost narrow enough to be a lane.

My beloved was sitting by a window, as usual reading about fairly recent local history while she kindheartedly displayed her something or other to everyone else who was present in the room – which is how I often think of myself in her presence.

Wishing to break a silence which sheer contentment was threatening to make oppressive, I gestured sharply once or four times and asked: what do you think the first organisms were like?

The first organisms on earth, do you mean?

Of course. For instance, you as you sit there – or even I, I suppose, if I must bring such matters into it – in almost every part of your body – not knowing they are there –.

What is the matter, she yelled, opening her eyes in such a way as to cause to disseminate through my own corporeal structure an insuperable spasm of what an orang utan would never in less than half a million years learn to call 'lust', which I managed to master almost at once.

Inside your body there are numerous small organisms – even

as you sit there – that object of yours – not knowing that you are in fact something like their enveloping planet – planet, hah! – my heart! my heart!!

Such simple beings – (I was not dead) – not knowing you are there – your laughter, for instance – that distant shower in the sky – even there – even in that explosion or orifice which unbalances the entire universe – I would rather like to know even better than I do now why it is that they are not shouting for joy – why are they not shouting from terror either? – why are they not shouting from a desire to stay where they are for ever?

Perhaps they are. We left. Shadows crossed the room.

(A sigh.)

Chapter 13

Perhaps, however, it is us who are the shadows. After all, I have of course, like most normal men, always been greatly attracted to cruelty in children. The sight of an infant thrashing away with a stick or a whip at some innocent flowering plant has always struck a delighted chord of response in my own being – particularly if I happen to be behind or inside that plant – and even more so if I myself happen to *be* that plant. This is so much rarer now than it used to be. As a direct natural result of this, there was a period of my existence when, whenever I found an injured bird on a bath – usually with a wing broken or otherwise impaired – I repeat: whenever I found an injured bird on a path – usually with a wig broken or otherwise impaired – I would gather it up tenderly in my hand and introduce myself on some pretext or other (as tax inspector; or escaped convict; or Anti-pope; or almost certified lunatic) into a suburban garden where the shouting of a potentially vicious child or children was audible. Usually, I would contrive, quivering, to place the bird near the child, and wait in tremulously pleasurable anticipation for it to see it (by which I mean, to see *it*), to scream with rage or disbelief or spite, and begin to jump up and down on the flightless avid, mashing the ignorant weeping volatile element to a pulp.

Chapter 14

In fact, usually this never happened. This never happened, usually. It happened once or twice. Instead, the ridiculously susceptible infant, tears habitually springing to his, or invariably to her, navel, would inexpertly gather up the much less than perfect feathery combination of base intelligence and irritating wing-flappings, and drift like a pleasant odour into the house to seek to induce a nearby mother – there is nearly always a nearby mother (ideally with pretty memories) – to tend to it. Thus, on all sides, we are denied our simple happiness in this world.

Chapter 15

I turn, stride out through the garden-gate with great dignity, albeit slightly hampered by impermanent physiological changes happening within me. Perhaps these are causing my teeth to erect? Not that one of you has to take my simple word for that: any observer will tell you the same, unless he happens to be blinded by irrational prejudices, as everyone is or are these days. I bounce through the streets until sunset, which, I have learned (for what is life or death or seduction without learning?), usually occurs at or near the end of the day, and the glory of which takes me by surprise as I am pulling the wings off a gigantic fly in Detah Street. I look up at the clouds and am astonished. Yes! They are above me again!

Chapter 16

Shortly afterwards, it begins to rain. I shelter beneath a tree. I am trembling with difficultly-repressed emotion. Above me, in the dripping branches of this custodial artery of mine or mind, a few perverts or baboons crouch, pretending to ignore me, merely because they do not see me. Flames of memory spread once more through the city where I was born, if such it was, consuming everything to ash. It was not Kilmarnock! Neither of them! Another moderately eventful day passes. In the evening, a flock of lame birds hobble past you as best they can, but neither their irony nor their bravery has the sightest effect on me. That, at least, is as it should be. One eye does not yet wait for the other.

Chapter 17

But, whether that is the case or no, I am waiting here for you. I accept that there was once another time which was not for you.

Not for you that I once sketched out a brilliant improvised theory about women being phallic symbols, then finally fell to the floor, drunk. I no longer drink.

Not for you that the River Mosel ran limpidly by the vineyards whence the wine had come, at 2 or 3 countries' distance. It still runs, or so they tell me.

Not for you that the white sheet fell langorously to the ground.

Not for you that an astonishing burst of music ripped through the air, so that everyone in existence felt a pang of regret that you had to be somewhere else.

Not for you that, in a room in the centre of Edinburgh, a young girl in blue is dancing.

Chapter 18

But all the rest will be for you delightful as a mild illness on a half-forgotten afternoon. Are you in the same city as me? Will our eyes meet? Or meet again? Oh, sweep away those hopeless atmospheres from the cluttered table beside your elegant arm, and put down there whatever tiny transient objects of inestimable worth you have just bought. I assume you have bought them. Turn your eyes towards me, but only if you wish to do so.

Chapter 19

The vision fades, and I am left with nothing. With even less than nothing, perhaps. Or, to be accurate, possibly I should say: with three-sevenths of nothing. Since there is no horizon, that cannot be dawn on the horizon.

Chapter 20

Can it be morning? The wooden gate is locked. A woman passes by outside it.

Various tame birds land. Now on this side of the wall; now on that side. As musical as absence.

Once again, opening and closing windows seem to be pseudonyms for immortality. Are you opening your window?

So long as no-one else is opening your window!

No-one believes in all these ordinary movements. No-one pays them sufficient attention. The woman is not there any longer. The same 2 birds still seem to be pecking about in the same space between the same walls. Yet the music in the other room is nearly 175 years old!

The grey light will not remain like this for ever. But it will stay for a long time, all the same. It tends to become blue.

Anyway, the walls are too high. Who can see properly over them? Not you.

Chapter 21

Ignoring the slightly inconvenient fact that this is not the world, I hurried on into the next room, and still she wasn't there. And so on into the next room. Are we a meal which a not particularly hungry universe – a glutton, in fact (let us not mislead ourselves by an inappropriate sense of politeness) – picked at and did not bother to finish? It went on to other things. It is, in short, insatiable. I ran down the few steps into the street. The thick fog of the previous evening had disappeared like the towel of a girl stepping into a bath. Not the least shred of it remained, and elsewhere the water slipped sideways in a million baths as enchanting bodies redistributed their weight. So why then am I here in this bloody uninteresting street?

I reached up a single hand and tried to grasp the morning, and it slipped between my fingers like a bubble as I had always suspected it might. But will anybody's hand catch it?

Chapter 22

Will anybody catch what? There is a hair floating in the air too. Does no-one else see it? It might be hers, I suppose. It might be what the stars form from. After all, they have to start somewhere, do they not? They have to form from something. Or do they have to form? Who are all these bodies, behaving as if they had to be here? All this blackness; this roaring sound. Am I the only one who hears it? Something is coming towards me from the left or the right; but not from both, not from both. Who is there? And, indeed, why? At least try to answer.

Chapter 23

As to myself: I would have been careful to train my wife and daughters (whom you are quite wrong to think of as being merely smoke – no matter how they started, or how they might end up) from the very first, to sit in a decorous manner, with thighs close together. For I well knew, from past experience with other wives and daughters, that if they, in a moment of possible forgetfulness, sit with legs ajar, all sorts of no doubt delightful but worryingly precarious birds will fly out of certain nearby spaces (which are certainly not those that you suppose), and will fill the air with glorious plumage and exhilarating aeronautical curvetings. But, finally, the senses become so dazzled by this pyrotechnic display of colour, freedom, beauty, throbbing, and intimations of a prelapsarian age, that one's intense inner happiness becomes a knife which threatens to castrate oneself. It then turns into a mirror in which one's possible daughters investigate their genitalia one after the other, in moments separated by slightly less than an hour. It then becomes a rubbish-swept bridge between two of the most desirable suburbs of the city, where neglected wives quietly whimper at night, as erotic or erratic as a large and obviously unreal bridge between two or three of the most desirable suburbs of the city, beneath which prowling dogs or photographers argue and contend over a discarded wrapping-paper, or comestible, or aperture, or head, or sense of the insufficient precariousness of life – such as certain neglected women feel at a glowing point in a decisive morning, when they are about to bounce their almost magical entities across a purely metaphorical bridge.

It next becomes the same bridge in the process of falling into the swollen torrent which threatens to fill a young mirror's brain as it examines itself with a sense of inadequacy opposite a young girl. The very mirror in which I inspect my newly donned public appearance before going out for another ordinary day's work! My head is surrounded by a halo of bright, closely circling birds all the way to the office, or department, or factory, or any other Friday mid-morning centre for a sense of the gross improbability of life. Such as a certain woman who is not being neglected or abused (will you not turn your eyes towards me twice?) feels as she touches her hair. Is she preparing to make a quick visit to a neighbour for a perfectly innocent and (indeed) laudible reason? She strokes her ear-lobes (oh, let my dead twin do that for you!), then fights an unwished sensation swirling or talking within her, then sits down, then separates her legs to let a large, at first awkwardly fluttering bird (whose first thought was not – "What? Am I extinct?") escape.

She is astonished to discover, not only that she has "created" such an unpredictable creature, but also that she has given birth to a steadily growing sea, which must in fairness soon (what?) be designated by the term "ocean" rather than "accident".

Chapter 24

A green door closes in a garden and the new sound of young laughter is heard behind it. Into this ocean landscape, after a century or two, flies the same fluttering large bird, now heading with what seems like unerring certainty towards its goal. It may be only a few seconds later – how can we possibly tell? The endless expanse of water does not appear to deter it in the least. Already it has flown for several years. Needless to say, in that time it has covered a great deal of distance. Its journey must surely be well advanced, particularly if it is flying in a straight line, which it is. It is not tired. It is not lost. It is not fictional. It is not going in retrograde motion. It is not in the least in doubt as to its final destination. In this it has the advantage of, for instance, me.

Chapter 25

Or do I, perhaps, have two destinations? Or, alternatively, am I perhaps merely a pair of destinations waiting to unite into a single quester? Do I hear someone else approach? No-one? No-one? Is that you?

Chapter 26

I am tired of being continually forced to pretend that I am me. It requires an expertise which I do not possess. Other people fill their spaces much more economically – and they also frequently have far superior reasons for walking on the other side of the road. This, of course, refers to a particular memory in Glasgow.

Chapter 27

However, let me try to describe it as it is, whether or not it is life. I usually wake up in the morning about six thirty, whenever the impressionable female whom I am exploiting by pretending to be unable to find accommodation elsewhere accidentally drops a cup of thankfully only lukewarm coffee onto my dreaming scrotum. Good God! Then I must still be male! I leap instantly out of bed: and hurry towards whichever of the world's trouble-spots it is that I am due to visit. Or, if it is Tuesday or Saturday, which it quite often is, I may simply stay at home, if the weather looks like being a bit rough, and perhaps potter about in the garden, or wonder what it is like to be inside a Chinese vase. Or I will perhaps look for some more antique Roman coins lost within my wife's throat – or in that of her sister, should she be visiting. Or in any of the other, more amenable housewives in this or in one of the immediately neighbouring buildings. (I would not wish to insult any of them by seeming to have favourites.)

I sometimes think think this would explain why I have so far married 17 times in all – were it not that I have never married.

Except perhaps once. But that probably lies in the future. Your eyes need not even look directly at me.

Chapter 28

Then, in the evening, I like to sit in front of a real wall – you know, a genuine blaze – with the dog, and the telephone, and the asteroid, and the tank, and the latest now. Perhaps I glower at a volume of moderately inaccurate history. My wife is cowering in the chair opposite, if absolutely need be, and is displaying to me all of her most crucial features in a fervent if doomed attempt to help me keep my emotional and psychological balance.

Oh, when such tight things were invented, God did not yet exist, but he certainly wasn't blind, was he!? Which reminds me.

That sudden, terrifying cracking sound all around us, as we open another bottle of Chateau Calvinblanc, whose label is different from what it was before (can we tell how?). One of our relatives or antecedents, perhaps sitting by the far wall, dies without a word, which is no more than we expected. Who was he anyway?

"What sound?"

Chapter 29

Then, in the next evening, everything is much the same. However, late on into the night, I happen to turn and look off out a window, over the back of my right arm, away from a shriek in the sky far above me. I see no-one on the road outside, whether moving towards us or away from us. A noise beside me – almost a cough – recalls my thoughts to the present room. Is she my wife? My wife has become almost luminous. The future seizes me around the neck like a kind but murderous creeper. The air falls down at my feet in little drops, moistening me slightly, ever so slightly. Let me stay like this always, I cry out.

I am at once moving towards the door. Do not let me pass through this door, I cry, as I inexorably begin to pass through the door. Soon afterwards, it is morning, and inadequate music is playing in the room beside me. Can this really be the very day that I had such terrific plans for? No; no; no. It never is, is it? Is this that life? I open the window, and a slightly familiar street lies before me.

Chapter 30

Why is it then that I can say without a vestige of a lie that I do not truly think I have ever seen that road before? Have I only one eye? No; no; no. Surely a normal patterning exists within my head?

Chapter 31

Inside what head? Surely there is no head inside which it is all happening? This funnelling together, this combination, this swimming towards an appropriate aperture. And that light! So much light! And you are here! You are here! Wonderful. Beside that window. Now only one question remains.

Chapter 32

Where am I?

Chapter 33

Furthermore, how can you mistake me for a laundry basket? And yet it is a simple enough mistake, I suppose. I occasionally watch you undress, and, oh, my uncontrollable yells of pleasure (I control them somehow) when you drop, with a nonchalance which an agency that had created almost 19 billion stars might allow itself to feel on producing yet another one (not noticed, not noticed, hardly even felt) more fragments of the historically fascinating and nowhere sufficiently recorded life of your underwear, into my capacious hold, which I toss and tear and worry, yet (eyes full of mature tears) allow you to pluck out with a cruelly cool hand, in order to feed the boring throat of a nearby humming washing-machine.

Chapter 34

I hope you did not think that that was me? You did, didn't you? Try to make less obvious mistakes, I beg you – for it is useless to ask you to make no mistakes at all. Let me explain a little.

Chapter 35

In this work, which I write solely for my own profit and pleasure – in which case whom do I think I am at present addressing? Well, I obviously cannot prevent any devoted offspring of mine – for instance, a grandson. Is it not astonishing to think that I may have a grandson? I often ask my grandson precisely this question, but he is as yet insufficiently mature to make me any helpful reply. But that is not the important thing.

Chapter 36

In this work, which I write in the hope that it may be of use to someone, at some time, probably in the future (which, like the past, does not exist, but, of course, in a different way) I attempt to describe as honestly as possible the circumstances of my life, in the hope that they may prove to be of value to someone, should anyone ever exist.

Perhaps it would be as well for me to begin with a few words describing myself. Although of slightly less than average height, this was not the first time that I had ever killed someone, perhaps a competitor, and I cannot deny the existence of spores. Nor would I particularly want to.

There have been few moments of stronger emotion, I need

hardly say, in the course of my entire life. Or there will be. The bleached bones lay by the side of the road for a long time afterwards, reminding me overwhelmingly of my second wife, whom (I suppose you have anticipated me yet again) I don't think I ever met. How could I? After all, I didn't even meet my first wife either. I have been appallingly unfortunate time and time again, but it is somehow not in my nature to complain.

Throughout my existence, I have been conscious of a strain of utter conventionality in my nature; a tendency towards almost unbearable boredom. Let me not claim that this is what I seek to recapitulate here. I have often unconsciously sought to make allowances for this, but I have never been able to achieve anything substantial. Some very dear friends have been kind enough to claim that my inveterate and increasing habit of breaking in through well-structured windows in the pleasanter suburbs, and attempting to find unfrightened women, usually pregnant (or in some similar state), who will be prepared to nourish me absolutely gratis (I categorically refuse to pay – after all, even I have my pride) with their absentminded milk, allowing themselves to be deceived that in this way the higher musical traditions of the civilisation of a slowly passing cloud-shadow called Homo Sapiens – but no. However, what Her Royal Highness said when, on opening the larger of the two goblets or containers, she discovered that I had in fact shat in it, I regret to say I was not present to discover.

Chapter 37

After all, that is not the important thing. The really important thing, I should say, is morning. Even though morning is simply a side-effect of women's knees moving. And the next morning is the same. What is that slippage and tremor in the air, if not an attempt at gaseous music; which is to say, fugitive kindness in neighbouring bungalows? Various doors open secretively, and various shoes or moons are put out onto the pavements, or perhaps gardens, by the doorstep. Of course, light continues to draw its lines indifferently over grasses, hints, motions and careful masonry. If everyone disappears, there will still be that same old game.

Chapter 38

Meanwhile, my dearest, I hope that you are still keeping yourself warm, whoever you may be, and that you will develop your heart until it is as capacious as that vast, ceremonious garden – with squares, fountains and itinerant killers – which ought to be right here, right here, outside my small chaste window, but the orders for which seem to have been hopelessly garbled in the lines of transmission.

Chapter 39

If I were morning, I would try to be less like a vain promise. I would try to be like the dreams of waking children, provided that it took them to an indubitable paradise, which it rarely does.

Chapter 40

Oh, I could forgive death anything, except its perpetual studied insult to women's navels. Yes; yes. Pour out more of the same old stuff. Is there anything worse than being an unsuccessful wave? Yet, where do the successful waves go to?

Into a flat, flat, flat, flat, half-lit, half-unlit, raging, totally pointless ocean. One more time and then I really must go. No. No. Really, I must. Anyway, I have to meet my mother this morning, and you have not.

Chapter 41

I have no further time to pursue stray thoughts, nor even (indeed) a brain with which to pursue them, though perhaps I am reminded of an incident of several thousand years ago. Let me not say several zilliphillion. No-one would believe it. Or, if they did, I would not tell them. Time is perhaps merely a graffito, picturesque as all those artists mothers – drawn, normally, with so much love. Or, sometimes, with so much indifference to all but the capturable lines on her hated old face. Viewers tend to suppose that it is love anyway, motivated by an unreflective charity.

And all those unpictured mothers beyond them! Who is not stridently relieved by their absence? We have too many images to deal with even as things are. Perhaps they wore too many clothes.

Chapter 42

It must have been more than two days ago now that I phoned my mother from a public call-box, to wish her a Happy New Year. So, a year must have started! (You may, if you are sufficiently rash, deduce from this that I even exist, and that there is such a thing in Nature as a year starting – I can hardly be held wholly responsible for your stupidities, can I?)

The coin-receiving mechanism was, inevitably, malfunctioning. So all I heard was a distant, recognised voice giving out her number to anyone who might happen to be calling. We were then, soon afterwards, intercepted by a loud noise, and cut off from each other. Rather like Life in general, eh?

Chapter 43

As I climbed the hill towards my disgracefully untidy room, it struck me that I would not be able thus casually to listen to her voice for an unending duration longer. Almost immediately afterwards – I am only guessing now, but I should say that it was far less than three-seventeenths of a century – it struck me that there was absolutely nothing whatever that I could do about it. Oh, most inadequate, unfilial offspring! Why do you not at once paint your testicles (if you can find them) black, stark black, as testimony to your perversity? Yet, there is sadness in this unjust world, and in a juster world there would perhaps be even more.

Chapter 44

I remember how, one Christmas (this is perhaps two Christmases ago), I was sitting in a chair in the corner of the living-room of my parents' house in Argsol (the previous owners of which, it has once or twice struck me, I know nothing whatever about – which is to say, even less about, not including their names), while surreptitiously hurriedly scratching down a few of perhaps the best lines of 'The Opposite of Non-Existent Women', when I observed that my father, balancing on one hand, on the couch nearby, had fallen asleep – as he has tended to do more and more often in the last few nanoseconds. Years – I mean years. I observed him closely for a colossal number of

picoseconds, and the whole thing grew to seem almost unut-
terably absurd.

That this man, who thought in German, with (as far as I
know) an admixture of Polish, and who somewhere deep in his
interior was still engaged in the Second World War, was an
immediate ancestor of mine. I observed his sleeping face, but
not his waving tentacles, slightly distended at the cheeks, yet
greatly dignified nonetheless. I shook my own head after a
while, not concussing the two asymmetrical walnut-like lobes
contained miraculously within it, somehow derived at least in
part from his, and I went back to my writing. What else could
I have done?

Chapter 45

I could have begun to masturbate, I suppose, but I detest
anything which smacks of the self-consciously avant-garde.

Chapter 46

Truly, if this room we were or are in had directly given birth
to me – and my ignorance of him was only slightly superior to
my ignorance of it – the whole thing would hardly have been
much less plausible. Who exactly do these nucleic acids think
they are, to cause us so much trouble? And to think that I have
a sister who is at present in Switzerland! I trust she has been
reunited with her luggage (misplaced at the airport) by now.

Chapter 47

By the way, I meant to suggest earlier only that all families bar one were assembled by pure chance, although almost everyone is too polite to point this out. In short: all families are the same in different ways. Or (to put a different point in a slightly different way), everyone is part of a secret society. That is to say, all happy families are unhappy in one of two ways – and, besides, are usually dead.

Chapter 48

Let me develop the point. All those children, running joyfully through hovels, or through smoky delirious meadows, whose atrociousness they do not yet fully recognise, and possibly never will – this is almost certainly true of their improbability – like the same child caught in different stages, still gloriously free of certain pernicious chemicals.

Or like different children climbing the same tree – ah, childlike indifferent ways – all childlike in different ways – but non-existent in an identical manner.

You do not sufficiently realise that deaths are like falling rain, each spot a different departure, but that infinite streets are now covered with clinging, immense uniform moisture. They stretch out, flat and wet, into the trafficless distance. Some patter against our faces. However, we all carry dead voices within us, and unless we are terribly forgetful we carry dead umbrellas too.

Chapter 49

Little escaping bursts of people pass in the street, and occasionally even a rank outsider can spot the similarity.
Or am I stationary, and is time being carried past me?
It is not being carried. It is passing.
Which is to say, nothing can pass without it.

Chapter 50

Something stirs in my ears, and I feel that perhaps I am about to understand history at last. Or am I only about to hear of it? Am I about to be able to assimilate perfectly the existence of past lives, and turn this comprehension to devastating advantage? Listen to me! Listen to me! Even you with those impossibly deep brown eyes! All will be as clear and powerful as the sunlight on that wall at the foot of which unbelievably normal though bright flowers grow. I hope they are not dead.

Chapter 51

Are they dead? And is someone now passing by behind that wall? Someone troubled? Someone mentally troubled? Someone carrying an object? (But what object? History? A heavy load? The past? A dead body? A tv set which works fairly well?) All of these at once, perhaps! But might it not also, or alternatively, be someone whose teeth are no longer in the pristine condition which it would have been so easy to keep them in? More or less.

Chapter 52

May I not jump up, as slowly as possible, and look over the wall? Can I not fly even to that ridiculously limited extent? The wind blows out the curtains, as if that were a sort of answer. I think I hear footsteps pass, but the road on my side remains empty. How unlike the road inside! I suspect that the recent passer-by was that closest relative of mine whom I never knew. A fine morning, with not the slightest chance of rain.

Chapter 53

Of course it is not morning. Such a term is of such limited local significance that I do not propose ever to use it again. More than that! I propose never to use it again. And, needless to say, I am still waiting. That beating which I hear (which I do not hear, but which occupies the space which, were it not empty or nearly so, would contain me) is presumably a heart. It is presumably not the sound of something deliberately moving towards me. Is something falling through the sky? But what sky? An arm? A torso? Unwanted memories of youth? Unwanted youth itself? And is it possible to fall through a series of gas-layers subsequent to a cooling rotation, before shriekingly landing in a room where a small group of people are sitting round a table at a meal so pleasant that they would otherwise in no way remember it? Are they looking up, wondering what that incalculable noise could be? Very well then. What is that noise? Has it always been here? Why do I not hear it? Has it always been there? Is it an echo? But how, tell me, can an echo always have existed?

Chapter 54

Have I always existed, but only as an echo? Or has there existed only an echo of me, but never myself? But you are my echo, are you not? Oh, of course there has always been an element of doubt about any personal existence. Thus, for instance, some claim that I have seven children; others that I have nine.

You are clearly my eighth child.

Chapter 55

But this hardly matters. The important thing is that, despite our mutual hatred, I have been a good father to them, whoever they are. I can actually remember the names of three of them on normal days. On days of exceptional acuity I have even occasionally risen to five!

Even so, their insane unreflecting rebelliousness appals me, as it always has done. It was for their own good that I forbade them to urinate for ten years. Can they not get that simple fact into their thick little skulls? Why can they not even try to understand either me or, failing a task so obviously far beyond their limited powers, that simple and perfectly reasonable hygiene-induced regimen? I know only too well what trouble such apparently innocent pursuits inevitably bring in their wake. Now, for my pains, they speak lies about me to strangers. And not always gratis.

Chapter 56

Were it not for those new, but by now apparently securely established bars down in the centre of this vast town, where human milk is available for a modest fee in a wide variety of sizes of container, my life at present would I suspect be one entirely without consolation. Not that I am in any sense dependent on such essentially frivolous resources. I could abandon it instantly at any moment without the slightest qualm. Therefore I have chosen never to do so. As it is, I suspect I am being immoderately laughed at behind my back.

And possibly behind my buttocks too. Nothing would surprise me. However, when the last one finally commits suicide – which should not be too long now, for I have devoutly persisted in giving the necessary subtle hints – I refer here, of course, to the last of my disgraceful ungrateful unnatural offspring – I would finally (joyful moment!) be entirely free of family ties, and I will be able to do precisely what I want to, at last. How many delicate knees tremble for delicious fear at that thought, even in the middle of this unlooked-for downpour!

Chapter 57

Or such at least was what the smoke thought, as it rose from the steaming backs of the horses up briskly towards the sky. In the carriage, our ancestors laughed. How they are laughing still! Squares of brilliant blue fell down about our heads, and smashed like spangles. Their warm, coiled interiors, flying over the surface of the road, had made a discovery which only became possible to the communications industry 500 or 1500 years later. Hullo. Hullo. Are you there? Can you hear me? Why did you say such cruel things? Panic? And in such a voice! What a voice!

Chapter 58

So: you wish to know where I am? Very well; let me tell you. It is a brilliantly lit corridor (it is mostly in natural light), where a hand holding something – perhaps a knife, perhaps a mirror, perhaps a year's ending – occasionally slashes up and down as if in despair. After a while, I run through the corridor. Time passes, needless to say. A dignified figure. A small, clawlike cloud, seeping forwards like a tiny electronic stain. By now we have lost track of any possibility of telling one end of time from the other. Two small objects now roll by – two centuries.

Chapter 59

Later in the evening, one of them rolls by alone. A brilliantly lit corridor. Someone, I think, is prowling around nearby, trying to find the electric switch which controls all this. At times, I think it is only one person. At other times I realise I simply cannot count up the number properly. However, when the garden outside blooms as beautifully as it does this morning, the limp flowers inevitably call to mind the penises of great men. This is what you might call an automatic reaction.

And the scent! The scent reminds us that, even four centuries or hours ago, there were already many women who were both attractive and uninhibited with one of their eyebrows, as a fairly direct result of which some of our ancestors withstood only with great difficulty the temptation (some of them succumbed to the temptation) to jump up and down in gardens not yet exquisitely in bloom. Not the most erotic of sights to outside observers, unless they had a sense of humour. However, there then followed the unexpected but quite unmistakable report of the hunter's weapon, or simple exclamation of surprise, and nothing was quite as it had been before.

Chapter 60

However, it would probably not have been the same as it had been before anyway.

Chapter 61

Now it is morning. An almost full glass of orange juice personifies hope as accurately as in any other universe, none of which I suspect to be possible. It lay on top of a nearby flat shining surface. Sighing with contentment, I (in the old sense of the word) ejaculated into her nearer ear.

My darling, I said (for this is easier than remembering names – of which there are so puzzlingly many for females) – and watched with joy her own throat contract in a terror of premonition or joy or whatever it was how should I be able to be certain what it was. Do you remember, I wonder, I continued, I sneezed, how once I talked about your unequalled body being an unquestioned breeding-ground for micro-organisms? This, of course, was no reflection on you personally, nor on your dead parents, let us not discuss this again, although it is in you personally that for me the problem, erm, the problem, the problem.

She suggested the word "culminated". Then she tucked in her throat slightly, swallowing some major universe which pretended futilely to be without important constituents. I was moved by this. But my eyes did not fall out, despite the fact that they were so close to some of her secondary sexual characteristics. I forget which. Also, I do not honestly think it can be proper to describe any of her sexual characteristics as 'secondary'. But none of that is vitally important, I don't suppose, for you or your totally uninteresting preoccupations which I ask your forgiveness for keeping you at all from. Let me weep nobly for a moment.

Chapter 62

Let me reprise. The first organisms on earth were of course far simpler than those. What do I mean by those? By those there, by those unseen, hidden inside your body where they at present are. I am not making a personal point. I am not still complaining subtly about the undercooked duck of yesterday evening. Was it even obvious that they were alive?

Who? The first organisms on earth of course! How often must I repeat myself? Not as often as they, obviously. They could not rearrange their hair, nor accidentally (if you can believe that) accidentally wipe clean a video-tape of a discussion about a possible miscarriage of justice which I was eagerly looking forward to watching, which all right all right I agree, is possibly a slightly ghoulish thing to want to do. Or might seem so to someone who knows nothing whatever about the subject. Why should anyone? I am not too proud to admit to myself, for I know that no-one is overhearing me, that instead I just watched her bum moving about for an hour or so, and let justice look after itself.

Chapter 63

But were they alive? That is the vital question. I suppose they were by definition. We must always be suspicious about certain things which are certain things by definition. It must be a most unsatisfying way of being alive. I should think. And yet, how simple they indeed were! What crude, unsophisticated structures! Granted, over colossal periods of time they tended to become more elaborate (different theys, eh?), and, indeed, they even learned or started to clump together. Let me sneeze again here.

At roughly this point I majestically climbed on top of her, while continuing to talk – for she has very often told me (at least twice) what a brilliant conversationalist she finds me under such comparatively intense conditions. I do not like to disillusion her in that way. Particularly when I can so disillusion her in other ways.

Chapter 64

Yes. From being colonies of separate individuals. Unimaginably slowly. What exactly is an aeon anyway? Developed into one individual with many astonishingly differentiated parts. Tissues. Where are they now? Organs. César Franck. Funny creatures running about in the blistering sunlight. Brain. The telephone. Fairly inevitable. The curtain flapping slightly. Summons. Disappearance. What a voice. The door shutting. The smile just before.

Or perhaps this here, which I think of as the other end.

Chapter 65

For, if I am at one end, surely someone else must be at the other end? Am I even facing in the right direction? But there is now a light shining directly into my eyes, and it is genuinely difficult for me to see what point there is in such things as (such things as!) sunlight existing at all. Unless it is to reflect off the bright pensive skin of girls stepping decorously through small bright decorative streams. As so often, this is external to that.

I grant them also the possibility of lanes, often empty for an entire afternoon, except for two people hours (or a single minute) apart. One of them I would not much mind seeing again. I mean, why else bother to light up the planet?

Or would it happen anyway?

38

Chapter 66

Are we seriously to believe in aeons of pure light; even in aeons of noisy little streams, with only an occasional scaly foot stepping briskly into and out of it, and then silence? Who is watching this? It is not me, I assure you. Believe me! Be reassured!

You are not telling me, are you, that the sky is full of such places and such lights? And not full of such streams? Or do you have the gall to pretend that it is full of such streams, but with no-one wading through them or underneath them – no-one remotely or, if so, not recognisably female? But why then have lanes? Why then open doors? I fear I have missed out something utterly vital here.

Chapter 67

In that case, one does rather wonder at the immense distances between them. There is little to be said, theoretically, for so much darkness. Oh, it may already have happened, or be about to happen again – but still there is little to be said for it.

Chapter 68

Smoke rises from the roof. The nearby factory clicks busily. Perhaps it clears its throat.

Soon the streets will be full of children going home from school. I must go out nonetheless.

Irregular cascades of them, thousands of bubbling capillaries, breaking out from different centres, becoming diffuse and intermingled, as one group interpenetrates the next, and so on, and the next, constituted rather as I assume my bloodstream to be, although I have been lamentably casual in bothering to research this and such things as this. But they too exist anyway.

Chapter 69

Yet, you would not think we could be surrounded by so much darkness. Why is it all there – so much of it? So much of it. Not where a group of children can barge round a corner shouting in exactly the way one recalls doing in one's own commencing youth, since almost totally forgotten about. Until now. And is she somewhere here?

Let us hope they manage to cure these lethal new sexual diseases which are floating about. Or, rather, which are in so many people's bloodstreams. But if this were my own bloodstream, it would be a room which leads into another room, which leads into a further room, which leads into a familiar room.

Chapter 70

Far below an intolerable expanse of water through which (at least) unfortunate people are falling, we sit dressed in our ordinary clothes, my hand on your shoulder. That is to say, you are trying to wear ordinary clothes, but you cannot actually do so. It is simply a logical impossibility for a perfect being to do so.

Of course, our fathers do not bump into each other in a remote doorway. They do not even look at each other. Our child realises that it does not exist, and leaves with impressive reluctance. We love it all the more for that. Had it opened its bowels for a second time that morning, it would have given birth to a surprised Greek god. Needless to specify which one. They don't exist either.

Our window loses itself in a row of windows, seen from the top of a nearby hill. Who is throwing these rocks at my heart? Some of them are monstrously large. Surely it is not you? Can it be? Is that the ultimate loyalty? Or is it some form of particularly unforgivable treachery? I forgive you anyway, as I am sure you do me.

Chapter 71

Actually, it has all happened so often that I begin to think that I may well in fact be music. Possibly music played fairly exquisitely inside a rare, Palladian building which, to judge from appearances, is empty of everything but the music. What is that which bisects the musicians? Is it Time yet again? Is it something which stands just beside Happiness? Is it an almost flawless proof of something or other? No: don't try to pursue it. It slips away with impressive speed whenever anyone starts to move towards it, even if only accidentally.

So you take off your dressing-gown and playfully drape it over my head. What scents! What darkness! What light! What arms! Oh, the discoverers of new continents were brave men, and I salute them, in a casual sort of way. But I do so from an inalienable sense of superiority.

Chapter 72

Not that I claim to be the only man – far from it – who has, at some point during his life, spent entire days blundering about with a large enveloping cover of some sort over his head. At its worst, it is an utterly opaque blanket-like construction, which greatly hinders my movements. When I finally manage to throw it off, I find I am in a low-lying part of town which I do not often visit, and never particularly wish to visit.

On better days, a certain amount of light gets through. And, occasionally, the obstruction can be so slight that for a long while I forget that it in fact exists – until my upraised arm, or that of a passer-by, brushes against it, silent as a disappearing empire.

However, I at least know that it is there – which is more than certain others can correctly claim.

Chapter 73

So why do women so often claim that I owe them something? Do they not realise how transient a thing the institution of money is? Perhaps if my eyes were completely detachable, I would be able to live a more satisfactory life. For I am at times almost tired of watching women approaching unapproachably through pools of light. Only very lately have I realised that they too die, still with their high voices.

So they too have not yet found a better plan! Mystifying, eh?

I am a moving spot in the eyes of a few of them. And something darker and more mysterious in the temporal lobes of fewer.

Chapter 74

It is all happening always on another level. Two days away. Three steps away. Never quite here.

It is all the same, except for a single opened door. And now everybody is five years older. We notice it particularly in the younger people – even though some at the nearer end have merely appeared *ex nihilo*. Is another gulp of fresh liquid as we peruse the still unsmiling image of an unspoken-to ancestor in a light than which light can not be more light unless somebody even more valuable than this light were sitting beside me, is it I repeat or continue a response adequate in weight to the expressions in some eyes? Well, is it? These are not small eyes that I am talking about, whatever she thinks. Or is it only examples of life that creep up to or through the open window?

Chapter 75

Perhaps I ask this only because whenever I see a pregnant woman (and there are always one or two freely observable) I am not always reminded of an open window. The reverse is not the case.

Chapter 76

I dare say if one looks very close up to a laughing child's face one does not see the sunlight flickering between the trees, even on a more pleasant planet devoid of life. But one may perhaps understand nonetheless, in a sudden flash of intuition (for what other sort can there be?) that history is just an unintentional by-product of dirty underwear.

I prefer my slightly non-existent wife to wear clean underwear, but the basic point remains unaffected.

Chapter 77

Look! Another child comes through the door. A mother (You?) playfully throws him something to catch. And look! A child comes through the door again! The mother (Not You?) playfully throws, or refuses to throw, something for *her* to catch.

However, the child catches it in any case. Where is the problem? Everyone is walking about with a covering over his or her head, but so powerful is the light of this morning, that for a moment all are fooled into believing that time is at last doing something which it has never done before.

As a matter of fact, it is – but not in the way that all of them suppose.

Chapter 78

After all, it is not so much the fact that happiness passes us by which disconcerts us, as that the feeling which we have immediately before we get out of bed, and those which we have immediately afterwards, can be so different from each other. Thus, for instance, the moon changes its attitude, losing its atmosphere and the endless chance of passers-by bumping into each other with cries of recognition.

Similarly, the mere fact that water has run here so often (even though up there it stopped doing so long long ago) is in itself less wounding than our knowledge that people entirely remote from us have wasted so much time in looking at each other.

Chapter 79

It is as if someone else were always sleeping behind us in the same room. In whichever room we visit. Or are.

Chapter 80

Just so. Though we stay there for years.

Chapter 81

We may die there too – what do they care? The light goes out. The window opens. Adoration too can become a mere matter of technique.

Chapter 82

Following the paths marked out for us, it is with a shock we realise they are no longer distinctly there. This led us in turn to worry about ourselves. We are absent too, aren't we?

Chapter 83

Beyond any door there is always gold light. I mean, there is always more light. It may seem golden of a sort, even though it is strictly speaking wholly ordinary. Is she there too? That people are inside the light is an accident of no importance.

She reached out a hand and touched me on the shoulder. I wondered where the other halves of our bodies were.

Chapter 84

Uncharted rivers chugged sluggishly (inside us? I suppose so) among exotic densities of trees.

We too, sitting in our rooms, were at exactly the wrong end of the planet for this. It is not for me to say that we were in an uncharted river of our own.

Nevertheless, I cannot help suspecting that innumerable pilots have sailed down the branchings of the aforementioned semi-fluvial quantity or strainbed or strained silence or entity, perhaps making superb and detailed maps as they went, but none of them has ever returned.

Chapter 85

Indeed, it is obvious that none of them *can* return.

Chapter 86

We are not expecting them anyway. And thus infinite information is lost, like time preserved during a power-cut, when women in the tall building on the hill not far away shriek at the unexpected darkness. Different shrieks from widely separate rooms, in none of which I am present. Let me say nothing of where I *was* present.

It is not me who walks over to them now, to pat them perhaps on the bottom, for reassurance or some such reason. Any reason is sufficient.

Chapter 87

For who could deny that all this was happening inside the egg which she dropped 3 or 4 mornings ago, breaking into a brief laughter herself which seemed the exact opposite of the spilled, smashed mess upon the floor? As for the egg inside our own bodies – if we touch that, the universe is forced to begin all over again. For is it not –.

Chapter 88

One moment, I beg you. Do not proceed so quickly. It was a thought thought only fleetingly, and now so long ago, but what did it mean? What was its significance, if any? Oh, year after year is thrown tirelessly at our heads, like eggs stowed somewhere or other – I can't be bothered crossing the room to find the exact word – surely it is enough to allude to the ovaries of a mature female? Of course, we were never such an egg. But something like us, a bit of us, something necessary for us, was.

What I would like to know is, I suppose, why these halves cannot lead their own independent existences. For I, like everyone else, assume they cannot. Do two viruses unite to form an accidental human being? My personal fear is that they imagine they are fighting.

Chapter 89

It is all so similar to a game of chance – a subject which I am uniquely well-placed to discuss. And this I shall do, just as soon as I have both, a: stopped typing a woman's short name over and over again on a friend's machine now that he has left the house, and b: done so a few more times, and c: walked over to a window and removed that apparently sneering or irate face peering in. Now. Where was I?

Chapter 90

Ah yes. I remember now. My passion for cardgames – one on which many fully-clothed people have commented – often with the light smile of nearly perfect incomprehension – is something which I must confess I might not have acquired on any of my many visits to the incomparable capitals of Central Europe, most of which, alas, I was forced to accomplish solely through the agency of photographic books, all of which contain many fully-dressed people. In those towns – one thinks here of Dresden, Vienna, Budapest, Largs, Breslau, Montreal, Glasgow, and so many Tripolis that one has difficulty telling them apart – I'll probably remove that later – it was my usual but not invariable practice to clamber high up the facades of buildings which had appealed to me for some reason or other. (No doubt they somehow reminded me of my youth, or I thought they might teach me the truth about eyebrows, or something like that.) I deliberately (it was no accident) sought out decorative architectural details which had perhaps not been seen for decades by another living being with a penchant for aristocratic noses and sophisticated electronic gadgetry which was by now verging on the obsolete.

To arrive in a city of other people, who talk the same bizarre language, and who can make their way (whether silently or not – and usually not) expertly to the local hospitals unaided, returns one instantly to some of the worst aspects of one's childhood.

Chapter 91

Everyone else seems to have been told things which have been unfairly kept from oneself. I am here too. I am lonely. I am tired. Help me!

Chapter 92

Always cry for help at least twice. That is one of the few infallible items of advice I can give you in this cruel world.

Chapter 93

But I remember now – I did once learn a game in either Polmont or Vienna. Ah, will I ever forget Vienna? It reminds me so powerfully of Paisley. But this similitude has already been commented on more often than it actually deserves to be. The game was called Quatonwatomfatombaton – a name, I believe, not of Hungarian extraction (meaning, I gather, something like, "Now It's Your Turn To Apply This Cucumber To The Queen" – but quite without any overtones of impropriety or cruelty).

It should be said straight away that it is, in essence, a fairly simple game – at its best when three players are involved, although two are perfectly adequate if the female is well-shaped. In addition to a normal pack of cards held together by a thick rope, one ideally needs a small bright room, a torch, a reliable map (the preWar ones are the best), three flat pebbles, a good lawyer, and an old lady who is either short-sighted or prepared to take staggering risks. She need not be religious, although it helps in one or two of the extremer predicaments. Never will I forget the astonishing circumstances in which I first learned the game.

What were they?

Chapter 94

Believe me: if I could remember, I would certainly not tell you.

Chapter 95

So, I had arrived back, neither beaten nor bleeding, in my rented accommodation within sight of Adalabarata Stafatara Strasse (which nomenclature commemorates the murderer of a major writer of the locality – this seemed to me to be a curious personage to name a street after, but more of that later) when I saw to my amazement that Frau Todund, my landlady (a quiet but evidently passionate female of, as her name suggests,

Greek extraction), instead of chuckling volubly, as was her wont, over a volume of Castanetti's apercus and witticisms, was lying on my bed with her legs shut. Her eyes may have been open; I do not explicitly deny that. For my part, I of course at once assumed that she was dead and began to embark on a fascinating course of social experimentation, such as would, I am utterly certain, have done a great deal to consolidate the reputation of, say, Lord Kames, as an *erforscher* of the ultimate subtleties of the human psyche. Such, however, was not how things in the end turned out. Did I mention that her sister was shrieking in Brno? Such a life-enhancing sound!

Chapter 96

Consequently, when Herr Ogurkenschnecke (who claimed to be her husband) returned just over three years – sorry, I mean just over three minutes later from his prolonged not unswinish wassail in the Bierkneipe, if that is how you spell the word, he found, whether he wanted to or not (and I suspect that he did not) that things had advanced to a voraciously interesting stage. By now, genuine passion – or at the very least, genuine loss of mutual indifference – was involved. I can still see him (in the mind's eye, Horatia – and also in this series of photographic studies which I have in my left-hand pocket) treading creakily up the wary stairway towards us, fearful of being discovered in a misdemeanour. As our foul luck would have had it, if anything like this had remotely happened in real life, he arrived just as the joust or partie was reaching a particularly crucial point. In fact, right at the Donkenswattteringsmoment.

Let me explain, for any recently returned astronauts who might require elucidation of this term. Here, the person with the fourth-highest holding (Sprnagbulo), unless by happy chance he happens to possess at exactly the same moment of play the Frnogucsi (a type of flexible rubber arm which helps to give the game its name and much of its point) – which is rare – can only

51

prevent the immediate loss of his or (more likely) her vonkuv by pretending to be a particularly affectionate (or, in some varieties of the game, intelligent) spermatozoon in as convincing a manner as possible. Verisimilitude is absolutely everything in this game, which you would be wrong to suppose is merely a metaphor for missed opportunities.

Chapter 97

Now, Frau Mita (it should be remembered) was a kind-hearted woman with an agreeable laugh, who demanded of foreign lodgers only that they made sporadic attempts to pay what they owed, and also gave her legs smouldering looks which they checked a split-second too late to escape her apparently inobservant observation. So she was always showing off her enlightened legs, and always apparently by accident. It helped to waft out an occasional overheard laudatory comment about the size of her eyes or the magnanimity of her fatherland. Or perhaps vice-versa, for like so many attractive women she had once been told that her eyes were too small, and had never been totally able to dismiss this as the nonsense which I for one could have told her it was, if she had been prepared to listen to me. Consequently, she was by now thoroughly drunk, or striped, or both – for the pleasing result of her reluctance to strop advancing intoxication was that she had stripped, or (which comes to the same thing) could be stripped with ease that she was strapping, every single game. Therefore, by the time her husband arrived (if that is who he really was), not only did she owe me 752,693 kisses on the vital orbs (and this was before the War, remember!)(what?), but she had exchanged her valuable house for a tiny thread which I had used to carry about with me, attached to my belt, as a good-luck charm. (I had found it years before in the clenched hand of a sleeping girl who had thrown over all the chairs not only her original clothing, but thirteen subsequent replacements too, and much of a fourteenth. I have changed, or invented, the real numbers.

But the chairs remain the same.) She was also trying to play the trumpet, and failing (though not miserably) in a manner liable to be resented by those favouring a more routinely accurate or traditionalist approach to music.

Chapter 98

After a moment or two's silent observation of this poignant scene, her dumbfounded husband turned – showing what I thought was, in the circumstances, an impressive amount of dignity – and reclimbed the stairs. As he did so, the trumpet accompanied his passing in a solemn melody of valediction. I interpreted it as a moving plea for tolerance. Golden days! We shall not gaze upon their like again.

Chapter 99

At least, I certainly hope not. (And I suppose you do too.)

Chapter 100

Nevertheless, if I were to nominate a single activity which has given me more pleasure in the course of my entire life than any other, I would probably be so eager to select from the area of all the more likely alternatives that I would forget even to consider the claims of that most enchanting of sensations – sitting half-dressed in a room which unmistakably belongs to someone else. This someone else is of course a woman, but I shall give no names, since such precision would interrupt the fluency of my lying. What is she doing, whoever she is? A horrible truth dawns on me. She is possibly examining the bedclothes for the lethargic descendants of certain urgent disgusting stains caused during recent nocturnal encounters. These involve oneself, though one is probably not the stain. How reasonably she is going about the task! How could we guess that what was involved here was primarily the very near miss of other creatures, complicated as ourselves? Who would think that this was the inflammatorily passionate and passionately wordless (by and large) creature of a few hours or minutes ago? Who would think she could speak very good German? Or is it Swedish? Or Latin? Or Polish? Who would think that her father – for he has lived most of his life moulded by that rash assumption – had his own large office (I might say, he still *has* it) which he had (probably) not yet reached? I ask her, at what time in the morning does her father begin his work? I am not particularly interested in the reply. Notice that I am careful not to ask her what this work is. This is not solely because she does not know. There are other reasons, which I carefully withhold from you.

Chapter 101

About now, she replies, and certain modest objects which I need not specify jiggle winningly and unintentionally as she looks up at me and then down again. Perhaps he is in a lift somewhere, himself looking directly into the neck of someone else, whose own or favourite or elder daughter – strange that what is so small – a shout – should also be unencompassable – a window opened – such opportunities – more opportunities – but I observe that my chastened member has almost disappeared. Who could truly blame it? For a moment, I panic at the thought that last night it was arrogant enough for an entire lifetime, and so I might well never see its shameless and ugly face again. Meanwhile, I learn from the newspapers that a few more children are dying in fires somewhere else.

Chapter 102

Outside the window, birds run up and down the branches of trees, like miniature noisy unconvincing centuries. Many cars pass already, carrying various cargoes of unhappiness, sometimes called children. Within two hours, I am walking down the street outside. Within 10 days, I am adjusting a bedside lamp in order the better to observe the – let me not specify precisely what, lest I be mistaken for another sort of pervert entirely – of a woman friend of hers, whom I would probably never have met – or not to such an extent anyway – had she not introduced me to her in a cinema two or three weeks previously. Curious how much is the same, and yet how subtle the differences!

Within five months, I am quickly crossing the road, and hurrying down a stairway to avoid her. On the day after, which is the first day of a new year, I am walking thoughtfully along the right bank (but this is ridiculous – surely I must mean something like 'the north bank'?) of a river in spate.

Chapter 103

Perhaps I am thinking of how stupid we are to talk of there being years orbiting neatly in the sky. Oh, they are there, I suppose – but surely only because we have put them there. We noticed; we drew the line. Not that the sky itself is timeless even before clocks have been invented. After all, clouds are a sort of clock. Anything that changes is a sort of clock. Where could time live, if there were no change? What could it inhabit? A heartbeat is a sort of clock; as is the noise of those bloody annoying children strengthening their psychological blackmail muscles on each other right outside my window; as is the emission of blood which contains or embraces an invisible but still material object which might have been half the strands of you or I or the artist of any good or bad anonymous painting or Aulus Gellius (no idea, no idea – have you?). Or of someone even less important, if that is possible. But a hand rests against a cool glass anyway; a head leans back against a cool tiled wall. Something is passing in a terrible hurry, and it may as well be time, however slowly it goes, which only very narrowly escapes sentimentality, if at all. Is she expected somewhere else in half an hour or so? And what was discharged then, and thrown away as a routine loss, too valueless even to be a loss? Perhaps that devastating beauty, not in the room beside me. Perhaps the eventual discovery of – but who will make that discovery now? We create some things, and do not create others. The same is frequently believed of God – a concept which does not even make sense. I pass on to more important things.

Chapter 104

It is obvious that we cannot say now what he might have discovered. How many possibilities women throw aside each hour. Millions, presumably. Obviously, the biography of a discarded ovum must, however fascinating, be cruelly brief. Autobiographies are, needless to say, out of the question. But it is intriguing to consider how very near the question comes to being asked. What do you think?

Chapter 105

I suppose it is most improbable that you believe that the year is at least one day longer than anyone else thinks it is, and that this extra day is itself full of empty heads? People disappear regularly on all the other days. Keys continue to be usable. Many of them are never used. Nor do we sit in groups of four round a table, whether inside the house or in the garden, perhaps because it is raining. The distance is still there, but it is not looked off into thoughtfully. Stop doing that, dear.

Chapter 106

Listen. The footsteps of a child may occasionally be audible, but that proves nothing. It is not what you were. Is it? Say it is not so; for during all those long years I do not think I ever once caught a glimpse of you. Nor should we be too surprised if the sound of a heaven being vigorously and impassively scrubbed clean is mistaken by we clouds for the sound of a divine being whispering far off. Or perhaps a car starting. Or perhaps both at once. Or perhaps the single thing which is the opposite of the pair of them.

Chapter 107

We do however agree, I assume, that without the word 'perhaps' the description of the universe would be unequivocally impossible. The same cannot be said about 'God', if you embrace in that term five million of the routine human fantasies of external agents. Presumably 'human being' is not utterly necessary, although I would be very interested to know what the dolphins, with their legendary wisdom, could tell us about television. Some, I suppose, will think that their ignorance of television is itself evidence of their wisdom. It is not for me to point out that the mind that would stoop to such a response is far less noble than mine.

However, 'brain' of some sort I would admit. 'Sadness' possibly. Clearly, 'vagina', or something like it (something like it!), is indispensable. But (perhaps) it is too difficult to linger here.

Chapter 108

Let us proceed at once to the ramifications, which are numerous. For instance, I doubt very much if the first reasonably hominid character who ever decked himself or herself, though probably not 'itself', out in a dead animal's fur, or a few large leaves, but not the neat blue waistcoat which I once persuaded you to wear just after a bath, for a wonderful ten minutes before you decided to start another argument, or did so without first deciding to, but did so anyway, did so, for what, why not simply accept that people are within your power without having to know exactly how much of your power they are in, or agonising whether or not it is sufficiently mature, conformable to the latest opinions in the most uptodate magazines, to nurture a precarious self-confidence by allowing teasingly unhindered visual access to practically the entire physical organism which you inhabit, unconfused by considerations as to whether or not your no doubt vast and unparalleled knowledge of the court intrigues of the Stuart kings, combined with an uncanny ability to know where on a map non-existent castles (now a mere knuckle or rock, or a sharp-cornered grass ridge) used to be – let me say here in my timid defence that I do not think that my grasp of history is inadequate – however fleeting were my opportunities of grasping it – anyway, she dressed (calling me a few choice names) and (growing more inventively vituperative by the minute) stormed out in her utterly adorable street clothing – had any idea (following on from "a few large leaves" in the fourth line or so) of how many centuries of manual labour, chiefly women's handiwork one supposes, would be the eventual result of this revelation, purely to keep clothes clean.

I am certain this was not the case.

Chapter 109

I am not referring here to the actual manufacture of clothes. You understand this at least, don't you?

Chapter 110

I see that of late we are developing machines which do practically everything as regards the washing of clothes – my own mother has one of these. One feeds in the laundry, presses a switch, and then goes away wherever one wants to, though rarely to the Meadows in Edinburgh. It whirrs, and contentedly follows its preset programme. 'Contentedly' was rather a stupid word to use. Would it have been better to say, 'tragically'? Perhaps like you, I neither know nor care. If anyone is content, it is not the washing-machine, which has never been known to smile. This is perhaps just as well.

Chapter 111

Let us think instead of false teeth falling to the ground. "False teeth"? No; I meant leaves; leaves. A peculiar mistake to make. Were I not an omniscient author, I would begin to fear that I might be losing my marbles.

Chapter 112

So: in little brick outhouses, a billion of them, seventeen women are washing clothes. Unpleasant, anaphrodisiac, spine-affecting, skin-wrinkling work. Strange, is it not, that this should result from a non-motivated (I speak here of intention) choice not to develop testicles while still a mere dot inside another woman's body, probably a dead one. However, one thing has to result from another, unless it is to be the same, and what exists has to be a particular shape, which need not seem convincing whatever it is. By the way, a very important man is riding past on the road outside. I do not consider it totally superfluous to add that he is on horseback. He is certainly not sitting upside-down on the horse's belly, nor is the horse perched on his own back in a manner calculated to facilitate motion. That would be stupid. Dismiss such pointless images from your mind. What was I saying? A few minutes later, another, similar, passes. It would be rash to suppose that cars need not yet have been invented. Of course, Jupiter (the planet) revolves around her or her navel as much as it revolves around either either man or either of either's testicles. The inanities of adolescent schoolgirls, as one of them stands giggling at a corner in a short skirt and a long open coat (I happen to know her name), shouting to her distant companion the following messages (which one would not have heard in the same place, if it had existed, 15,000 million years ago): "No! Don't! Come on! Come on!" – I could not quite work out what her companion (invisible to me) was threatening to do, although I think two boys were in the offing – their arms move as bizarrely as did those of Schubert. Is "bizarrely" the proper word? (I refer, of course, to Schubert's brother, Ferdinand.) Meanwhile a duststorm surrounded by years of emptiness tells us, though not bizarrely, that everyone is central, or that everyone is at the circumference. It all comes to much the same thing, particularly if there is no-one sleeping nearby, whose little breasts we can watch moving until we are simultaneously aroused, filled with love, and terrified pretty well beyond speaking. So that is what they're mainly for, is it?

Chapter 113

As I was saying, the leaves are falling to the ground. There is a woman cleaning clothes. Each soapsud is history. The roof has fleas. The dilapidated dog has long since collapsed, shattered by thunderstorms. Men are carting away rubbish in the narrow lane outside. Their noise would disturb the famous writer, were he not at the moment in a pleasant hotel-room in Paris, sitting at a window, watching an occasional hat pass. Yesterday, he did not know that this room existed, and did not feel its absence, and therefore he was not at present wondering why it does exist, as it certainly seems to do. But what next? When in doubt, as James Young Simpson put it, usher in a few pregnant women.

Chapter 114

Across the road from his window, pregnant women are wondering what to do next. Inside their bodies, other people almost similarly wonder. Such future wonders. Three boys playing in the street outside scream at each other in depressingly accurate French, then fall through an unsuspected gash in the air into another life, forwards backwards or sideways. Neither they nor their antecedents understand each other, of course. And the same for their descendants too. How could it be otherwise? Yet; it could be otherwise.

Chapter 115

Well, actually it *is* otherwise. For, neglecting the light that shines through the window onto the empty chair, observe the large flightless bird continue to fly onwards over the ocean. It has, as I have already said, already done so for several centuries. Actually, the manuscript quite clearly says 'years' here. It obviously knows exactly where it is going. All this water buffeting to and fro, or changing its mind and moving relentlessly in one direction. What of all this liquid? The bird flies by again.

It is not in the slightest worried by, or even interested in, the utter absence of fishes. It is confident that one universe will not be succeeded by another. For what would have to happen for such a thing to occur?

Chapter 116

It continues to fly, and the water continues to flow beneath it, until the child is at last persuaded to open its mouth, and it drinks in one gulp the whole of the healing draught or medicinal concoction. With an expression of disgust, it hands the glass back.

Chapter 117

Relieved, the mother soothes the perplexed infant, using words which make mild illness seem a necessary, indeed laudible, almost desirable, hardly gaseous, part of the universe to which both of them probably equally belong. Outside the porthole of the cabin in which the two of them are sheltering, if they are not in their home in one of the back streets of Greenock, the same sea surges calmly past, singing a Tyrolean folksong. A dead bird plummets into it out of the unclouded sky. The sea flows on. Calm, disconcertingly solid, slightly plagiarized, and infinitely deep.

Chapter 118

It is almost as complex as – and certainly it is a necessary precursor to – the mind of a man who, after an evening of moderately successful entertainment, is in increasing frenzy struggling with an elaborate feature at the back of a woman's dress (the woman is still inside it, fairly hopeful – albeit, she trusts, not unrealistically so), while the nude light of an audacious moon glints on a watch on a window-sill next-door. In beauty, it (that huge lump of floating airless rock) can be compared to the spectacular flowers in a vase which the previous person but two in the room surreptitiously removed, or to the woman's threatened but hidden armpit. The dazzling light is similar in all cases. Excuse me for a moment, while I score out the word 'clitoris'. This is something which I have found myself doing depressingly often recently.

In intensity, it can be compared (inaccurately) to the brightness in the room, or to the intense, serious wish of the male that his penis will soon at long last begin to mimic a quite different phase of the Roman Empire from that which at present it seems to be content to imitate.

In glory, it can be compared to the irritation on her sleeping face, or to the absent moles of her mother, adored by someone who has just lost his keys, and is standing distraught at a door.

(Don't worry. Someone is standing on the other side, all too ready to open it at the appropriate moment.)

Chapter 119

Anyway, the sky or weather continues to beat down. It revivifies the sea like a mother nursing her child while her husband tries to make contact with her nipples from Hong Kong. How strangely all is suffused at the moment by the thought of a woman who is absent. Why are you not here? Do you not know how much I am waiting for you? My longing for you is entirely unlike a burning curtain beside which obscene songs are rotting like the last ebb of a sea into which a devoted chair is pushing a woman who mistakes it for her son. To suppose so would be to mistake my motives entirely. Of course jealousy is involved. Jealousy warps the mind so that it becomes devastatingly like a dog barking when it sees a golden week of other people's mutual awakenings in well-serviced rooms, lurking in the shadows of such beautifully scented bushes rather like rhododendrons across the road, the wide road, the wide salt unplumbed steep estranging footstep-endangered road. It is also very like the sea above which a particular heart-stopping anguished object is flying, but that is surely too obvious to mention. I should have forgotten to mention it. I dare not be more explicit.

Chapter 120

However, since the subject has so naturally arisen, I may as well in my fictional guise confess here that the attentive look of a mother cuddling her sweet-scented child against her similarly scented cleavage is one that I have never tired of chancing to observe – particularly through a window fairly high off the ground. Nor is that similar look which she gives when the child is absent. This may sometimes be towards her navel, of course. Proper timing is vital here.

Chapter 121

And then, of course, there is also the look of a mother glancing involuntarily upwards towards a higher level where her child lies sleeping (or so she hopes) – perhaps (although this is certainly not necessary) while with malicious good nature her husband's normally somewhat choleric boss laboriously but successfully penetrates something which is not her consciousness, while groaning a fairly nondescript remark about Livingstone. An understandable association of ideas, I dare say. It is casual delights such as these which have done much to give allure to the drabber passages of my existences, which last word ideally ought to be in the singular, shouldn't it? I ask you, because I am sure you are exactly the sort of person who, if only you can be persuaded to stop betraying your better self by holding certain areas of your psyche to be immune to criticism, would notice such things.

Chapter 122

Where, indeed, would we be without the family?

Chapter 123

I recall an afternoon not of ten or so seconds ago, when I wandered in a leisurely manner out into the garden of the house which I was staying in (unknown to most of the other occupants) at the time, and I discovered to my surprise, but not to that of Robert Burns, a distinctive physical object, who had died almost two centuries previously, that on the lawn to the right of the path there was a gentleman lying prone, blood or memory pouring from a head-wound, or that, some way further on, to the right or left of the path but not both, there was a girl anxiously wondering what was going to happen soon to her incontinent mother. I mention this because the future is a light shining on an untrodden path. (A natural light, do you think?) Perhaps she had just grasped for the first time the true simplicity of the concept of time, which so many persisted in misunderstanding by considering to be otherwise.

Chapter 124

Gradually returning to the house, I at last heard the terrible news of the Portuguese earthquake – though not of the recent chronic inconsiderate suiciding from the spires of Notre Dame, who landed on an innocent or fairly innocent 14 year-old schoolgirl and killed her too, without even having been introduced. One could scarcely imagine a grosser breach of etiquette. How could this be possible, I asked myself, taking out of its hiding-place in the slightly battered but still service-able ornamental skull which I keep as both a paperweight and a conversation-piece on the shelf nearest to me (yours, I believe?), my collection of extremely sensitive photographic studies of the still quivering buttocks of 19th-century females who could speak Arabic, and who once usually did, though now, whatever continuing living emotions they inspired (for my part it was a mature ecstasy two-thirds as intense as the average of their fathers-in-law's religious faith), surely now moved their so learned little tongues no longer.

Chapter 125

These images are of no particular significance to me, even if they did once cause a murder. Murder is frequently trivial. No: this *sammlung* is merely one of the memorabilia I acquired at random during the course of existence – much like this unused telephone, this lock of hair, this marked sheet of tissue, this occasional sense of unutterable bafflement, or this blindness in one eye, which I first noticed during a quiet period of the last war. What stirring times they were, were they not? It changed me utterly. I for one will never be the same again. Now at last I began to understand history. Ever since then I have been peculiarly reluctant to believe those who sought to tell me that such an entity in fact could not properly be said to exist.

Chapter 126

Actually, I may as well confess that I had a rather quiet time during the last war. Nor would it be entirely honest to say that I had won the previous one single-handed. In fact, I had a very quiet time during all the wars in which I took part. I prefer to attribute this to my military genius, which is sometimes described as speed of foot. It is certainly not the result of cowardice, a failing utterly unknown in my family under normal circumstances – except where my Uncle Hector is concerned, and even here I feel it would be fairer and more accurate to talk of sheer absent-mindedness. Which of us has never been absent-minded? It is very easy, when under stress, to forget such superficial distinctions as that between right and left. After all, would there be a right and left in the universe without us? (Think for a few years before answering that question. In the end, excessive haste defeats itself. Why must it not be the case that the universe is an infinite or nearly infinite labyrinth with no centre?)

Chapter 127

Nor, actually, do I see how it can be possible to talk of love, of real love – love tried and tested – between a man and a woman, except where the man has spent several weeks – ideally, it would be over 37% of a lifetime – living in a narrow sparse room beneath the floor on which the beloved walks. Occasionally, perhaps, he steals out to watch her sleeping or weeping. This is largely a matter of luck. And, as a last resort, no woman can be entirely indifferent to a man who has eaten her chair in the attempt to prove his love for her and the ferocity of his jealousy. Conversely, no woman can ever really love a man who has killed an octopus by jumping on its head more than once. But that is by the by.

Frankly, to me such behaviour smacks of desperation.

Chapter 128

The furthest depths to which I personally have been forced down into in the agreeable insanity of the amorous affection occurred when I had the great good fortune to fall in love with the devastating daughter of F.X. Trugotrodnic – the brilliant author of The Hidden Pendulum, The Hidden Vulture, and This Is So Hidden That We Don't Even Know It Is There (the last published in the USA as Ultimate Secrets Exposed). What a mind his was! I always am – I mean, I always used to be heartily welcome at the comfortable and civilized home of that extraordinary man, who had the gypsy in his soul – and frequently, alas, had the gypsy's wife hidden somewhere in the bedroom. I will excise this later, and mention instead that his sole weakness, to my knowledge, was an excessive fondness for hallucinogenic soaps – a foible for which I would certainly be the last to upbraid him, since (quite apart from the fact that this is a vicious slander), under their hypnotic influence, after twenty or so litres, he seemed to me to be exactly the same as before, except on the rare occasions when his tongue flopped out in a civilized manner and he went concomitantly blind, a set of circumstances which enabled me to talk unhindered to his at times almost too cruelly ironic and contemptuous daughter. Oh, there is something dreadfully intoxicating, nonetheless, about an excessively rational woman!

The unpleasant smell, however, is probably what led to the distressingly early death of his wife.

Chapter 129

I need not develop the point. It is futile to attempt to be rational with a woman who is dead.

Chapter 130

It is not for me to speculate on why he insisted that she should always appear at the table in the mornings in attire suitable for a prostitute imitating a nun. What man does not have these or similar irrational preferences, doubtless implanted in him in childhood? This does, however, suggest to me that his much-vaunted religious orthodoxy was sheer affectation, or, at best, lightly-worn. In this connection I recall a typical and favourite remark of his to the effect that faith in God is literally faith in Nothing, with a capital N – a remark whose accuracy is beyond doubt to all but the most committed surrealist, but which I nonetheless felt showed a certain lack of religious faith – as that particular socially-condoned irrational prejudice is so often called. However, if he taught me nothing else, I learned from him that it is perfectly possible to live a long (say 83 years) life of mendacity and evil, and to die applauded by the community, who immediately waft you on their wishes straight into their preferred nonexistent Paradise. He was a brave spirit, and one of my dearest friends. I still miss him deeply, whenever I am accidentally reminded of him.

Chapter 131

However, in due fairness to the memory of the deceased, I wish to place it solemnly on record here and now that I never even once took advantage of any of the numerous opportunities which his saintly wife used to give me to make a variegated cuckold of her husband.

Chapter 132

His daughter, on the other hand, I once saved from drowning. A terrible death – even in a fiction which exists solely because I refused to abandon several past totally failed works until I had managed to wrest something out of them which I could slyly land on an all too trusting publisher. But this is a secret, and I certainly hope no-one intends to go about repeating it in the wrong places. Show some consideration for literature, I beg you. Anyway, I dragged out her besieged body from the inundating element, proceeding to heat her up beside a fire which was fortunately ablaze nearby. I forget why. There was probably a reason originally, but as one changes details one inevitably starts losing track.

I whispered in her ear that I loved her, which perhaps was taking unfair advantage of her bedraggled state, but, like all normal men, I have never been entirely able to shake off the allure of half-drowned women. For I have never for a moment believed that a woman is a card-trick – and certainly not one where someone has played out of turn.

Chapter 133

She turned her large, suffering eyes towards me, and for a terrible moment I thought that, despite the precautions I had taken, she might actually have seen me push her into the flood. But no. All was well. She leaned over tentatively towards me, opened her mouth a little, and directed towards me a considerable stream of water. This lasted for some 25 or 30 seconds, all told. I interpreted it as gratitude. Feeling rewarded by this far beyond my deserts, I realised that the time was right for a noble gesture on my part, and I boldly showed her where it was that I had hidden her clothes.

Chapter 134

After this, her behaviour towards me changed considerably, for, despite what Lord Reith might have said, no woman is an automatic vending machine.

Chapter 135

Do you wish an example? Yes: I am speaking to you, whose face is at present covered with a smirk of ecstatic gratitude. I did it merely to catch your attention, for I intend to give you an example anyway. Consider this. Let me instance the moment when, wondering how it could possibly have got there, she took it out of the cupboard and slipped her foot into it. She had another foot too, you understand, but every attempt at history is perforce partial.

Yes, I shall certainly continue with this after all. So, she looked through the hangers for the dress she wanted and, finding it, rather than one of the lost works of Tallis, she withdrew it, giving a repressed cry of triumph. To my joy, and also perhaps to my surprise, I discovered that the skirt was in fact me! Oh, there are some delights too great to be talked about, even though books must continue to be made, I suppose. (Particularly so if one is an inanimate object.)

Chapter 136

Of the next few hours I remember little anyway.

Chapter 137

Perhaps the ecstasy of light rearrangements of a body, while nearby a semi-bearded semi-fool droned on about profit-turnover ratios and the views from various rooms in Alicante. I admit that it crossed my mind to wonder whether he was actually real. Why should an entity so uninteresting be allowed to drift so near to her orbit or orifice and linger there?

Chapter 138

Once he even had the temerity to touch me! She thinks it was an accident, but I know better.

Chapter 139

It was only with great difficulty that I restrained myself from biting his finger off. Perhaps I remembered just in time that a skirt, however attractive and of whatever colour, just does not have fingers. Or do I mean 'teeth'? Women, however, have fingers, which is what keeps distracting me here.

Chapter 140

Now I lie, still slightly dazed and delirious, on the floor. Is this a carpet? How long have I been here? Should I perhaps leave? Can it be time to go? Since time exists so tenuously, how can it order me about so imperiously? Oh, how few good women there are in an empty room! Is this room empty? Is it time for me to go?

Chapter 141

Yes. I must reluctantly conclude that it is long since time for me to leave. So: I begin to inch my way towards the door. (A skirt inching its way towards a door! – that is something one does not see twice in a lifetime.)

Of course, I have not yet achieved the capacity for opening doors, and so I must wait beside them like an inferior form of life – a bored cat, perhaps – idly or morosely or impatiently flapping my pleats if I have any, until someone else is kind enough to do so. Fortunately, after only a few minutes, the door opens furtively and a strange, suspicious-looking man enters, no doubt a neighbour of some kind.

Chapter 142

I hurry out into the hallway. I creep on, in a motion perhaps rather like a caterpillar's, towards a richer world of colour and excitement. How like a caterpillar all round! I have often heard rumours of this. Indeed, I have often caught glimpses of it, insofar as I can honestly be said to have eyes, but I have never yet fully seen it. Even so, I too am part of this universe – do I too not deserve such a taste of its ultimate joys? I am often told that it should surely be enough – more than enough – that I am allowed – indeed, encouraged – to pass so much of my time hanging on her body – and that others would give a decade for ten minutes of such humdrum unbearable bliss. Why do people so insist on casting up to me my single inadequacy? I tell you, it is not even a genuine inadequacy. Consider the alternatives. We should be applauded for our almost saintlike self-abnegation. If we skirts were intelligent enough to know what we were clinging to, clothing emporia would become the sites of wars too hideous even to contemplate. You will note that this is inconsistent with previous passages. But I cannot continue with this fruitless digression, for I can now quite clearly hear footsteps approach which are obviously those of my returning owner. Where can I hide? Obviously, I do not wish her to discover me. I know exactly what she will do. You cannot cling to a woman's backside for six consecutive hours without being able to form a pretty accurate estimate of her character. She would utter a brief curse, and cruelly, summarily curtail my inevitable forward march to freedom. She is, I fear, so terribly middle-class about such things. She has so little instinctive understanding of the rights of the exploited. After all, I don't see why I should hide my political views from anybody. I have as much right to them as anyone else. Why should I compromise?

Chapter 143

Just in time, I manage to slip into a narrow sparsely-attended cellar below the carpet. I hear her footsteps pass above me. These are my ears here, can you not see them? She continues on round the corner to the left – yes, that is what I mean – and, having reached her door, she stands momentarily in front of her – no: I mean, of *it* – searching for her keys. Keys are something which she often searches for; unlike, say, nipples, which she usually leaves others to search for.

Chapter 144

Within a week, she is inside the room. She crosses almost at once to the window, looks down to the street below, checks that all is clear, and begins (in a leisurely manner, I suppose) to alter her apparel to a normal extent commensurate with the informality of being at ease in one's own apartment. And I am not there! I, who am not a skirt, am not there! In the wrong place again, as per bloody usual.

While so doing, she abruptly stops – and it is difficult to stop doing something unless one is actually doing it at the time – and holds her head to the side, as if listening to something which is not my tears, alerted by what seems to be a noise coming from the direction of the nearby cupboard. She goes over to it, and, frowning slightly, opens the door. To her vast surprise, she discovers that no-one is there.

Chapter 145

Yes. Once again, I was not there. Even when the likelihood was so comparatively promising; even when I myself was in command of the details; still I was elsewhere. The stupidity of this smug room appals me sometimes, as indeed does the new colour of the paint on the door. Or do I perhaps mean, the colour of the new paint on the door? It makes little difference.

Chapter 146

Have I still not settled where it is that I am? But if who I am is still not settled, then how am I to be able to decipher my exact position? There is a logical riddle here which not all the greatest minds or parts of minds, thinking it out in unison, which is impossible, will be able to get near to. Who can be surprised then, that they all turn in unison to self-abuse?

Chapter 147

Let me, likewise, change the subject, albeit in a somewhat more decorous manner. One soon grows accustomed to such vast, magnificent halls, and one soon forgets the feelings of awe which they originally inspired in one when first one encountered them, a raw youth. (Not a raw steak. I see no reason to suppose that a raw steak – or, indeed, any other sort of steak – ever experiences genuine feelings of awe. Controversial, perhaps; but I shall not dissemble my real opinions in the pursuit of easy applause.) How accustomed everyone else already seemed to be to them then! But now I find myself trying to make myself aware of those other eggs who are still unsure of their surroundings. They blunder into the wrong offices, or accidentally find themselves to be on window-sills, hands, floors, sheets of paper, and so forth. I cannot deny that, for my own part, I dislike opening windows, for of course the action always keenly reminds me of my late wife. Even now, even now, I cannot believe that she has fallen into the sun. All the same, since that must be where she ultimately originated, there is at least a certain symmetry, if a limited charm, involved in these arrangements and rearrangements.

Chapter 148

To continue. The afternoon seemed so unassuming, cowed by the suppleness of all our arm movements. Our cat or our lives sprang into the air, but did not stay there for long. Where the air itself went to, I do not know. All we can be sure of is that the penis of sorrow is less erect than the clitoris of joy.

Chapter 149

I, or perhaps my son, soon came down the stairway carrying a few books. A being for whose existence my penis was at least partially responsible, but not his, not his – let me not too closely invoke all that staggered wagging in the past – was standing beside the nearby cupboard saying "boing boing Boing". This is not an exact transcription, and I do not read any great significance into the particularities of the phrasing. What matters is that the present determines the present.

Chapter 150

But keep the cupboards shut, for God's sake, lest any dinosaurs escape! They have already done so so very often already. Have they not? Or, if not them, their similarities.

Chapter 151

Already a small pool of water has crept out self-consciously onto the floor.

Chapter 152

It cannot be the love of a mother for her child, can it? Can past hours be taken out of a cupboard – yes, that cupboard there – by her not necessarily red chipped hands? Some of them are plastic or unreal, but we do not know that yet. Who will ever be so heartless as to tell us that? Perhaps those who never find out at all are the fortunate ones. And then the world naturally splits into two worlds, and we find, naturally, that it is the wrong one that we are in.

Chapter 153

Nonetheless, unabashed, after a gap of 16 years, I opened the door and walked back into the house. We all know that momentary feeling of certainty of having learned everything. We all know it and we almost all forget it, though perhaps not deeply enough. Let us proceed.

Chapter 154

Here I am, my darling, wrecked and trapped on this half of a life. Will you not even try to come and rescue me? Grief rubs my toes, the sky does the same to my fingers, and the past approaches like an attractive human being weeping convulsively in a skirt which has recently been destroyed. We will soon enough reach the period when only the stars dance together. Why should we be in an accelerated hurry to get there? And still we persist in ruining so much in order to produce utterly unreadable books.

Chapter 155

People are passing by on the opposite side of the road and do not look towards us. At times we suspect that it is clear that life is a stairway between the mouth of one sleeping aperture and another – or rather, to be more precise, that it is not an extinct type of dog barking in a way which fails to affect the nearest thing to menstrual blood in an edible underwater protozoon, whose religious beliefs enchant the moon which is sliding down the expanding sky, becoming harder and harder, and colder and colder, and losing forever now the possibility of a light mist at the top of a suburban hill near a particularly valuable open window, through which anyone passing below with exemplary silentness might, if he were more fortunate than surely any reasonable desert could merit, hear such an enchanting voice emit perhaps a single light low cough, which is more music than the whole earth could have been predicted to hold. If you take my point.

Chapter 156

Some women are sighing in most cities, and turning over on their sides. Is it possible that you are unwell? How can she possibly be unwell? If so, then know that, within an hour's journey, a million fitter people move about, with remnants of already largely forgotten meals dripping deeper into their interiors. Thus the pregnant walls of the cities give birth to half-wrecked hopes, which struggle indomitably to meet each other. Never can they quite rid themselves of the fear that they are answers to unasked, perhaps even unaskable, questions. A question does not guarantee an answer. The neatness of so many of our books perhaps misleads us in this.

Chapter 157

The ill day towards its routine end shivers with cold. It draws up around its neck a cover lost up a lonely stairway in the underwear of the suburb. Meanwhile night, the doctor, races mindlessly after a stick which a deaf astronomer has thrown off into the obscure distance with unfamiliar cries of encouragement and glee. Throughout this town, which may also as well be that town, families are sitting down to meals, or weeping, or doing whatever the hell an ordinary and impossible thing it is that they are doing, while something fairly threatening (is it cell biology?) is creeping up behind contentment, carrying a large bucket half-full of a liquid which at first sight looks to be mere water – as if there were such a thing. It is for us to itemize the additions to this fluid and their extrapolations as far as we want to. Do we want to? Not many do. Or such is roughly what I took the nearest birds outside that magical window to be singing. And I would like to meet the person who can prove that I am wrong. Which is a hypocritical remark, if ever I heard one. Keep your non-existent proofs to yourself.

Chapter 158

But if we are to call the monotonous sound that these birds make 'song', then what are we to call a woman's sighing, was the thought which continually reverberated through my brain, or through my uncle's brain, as he, or I – dammit, I incline to think it was *he*, for throughout all this time I have been sitting in the garden, talking in a mixture of sunlight, mature resignation and leaves to the mother of the woman who for a miserable part of my not entirely miserable life I, to be quite frank, worshipped. A quiet street reclined on the other side of a moderately high wall, partially covered and/or obscured by foliage.

Chapter 159

Both of our brains contained enormously subtle assemblages of thousands of millions of interconnected neurons. Neither of us knows what a neuron is, of course, although *I* think I do. Nor did we even, either of us, begin to grasp intuitively the immensity of time which was necessary before such things could contrive to develop from the witless entities which accidentally started replicating in the sea. Oh, ignoble fornicators! That such should be the ancestors of us, who can sit looking at each other's eyes for hours!

Chapter 160

Such anyway was pretty well what I said to her, leaving out a few hints and witticisms and mildly flirtatious exaggerations which may even have required her eyes. Although she at first favoured me with the sort of glance which one might well choose (for whatever reason) to bestow on the only mammal so far developed – as far as I know anything to the contrary – capable of throwing an English literary magazine out of the window of a moving train somewhere before Kilwinning, she eventually became restive. It will not surprise you to learn, however, that we have also developed techniques for dealing with such minor and transient emergencies.

Chapter 161

Consequently I picked up a nearby pebble, and sought to entertain her by trying to estimate its age as wittily as possible, not without the intermittent use of my own sadly unprehensile lips. Being devastatingly amusing about little pebbles is a challenge I relish. However, she merely lay down on her side, groaned once or twice, and eventually gave birth.

Chapter 162

This caught my attention, of course, and I did not hesitate or scruple to make that clear. Of course, I said (and I do not claim that this is an original remark, though I must in my defence say that I can no longer remember where it was that I stole it from) that the question of how organisms per se may have originated is still intensely controversial and is currently, is it not, the subject of wide-ranging researches. What do you think? As if in response, her daughter stood up sharply and looked round. She winced inwardly at the garish exterior of a neighbour's newly redecorated house. As to what the neighbour was doing – who knows?

Chapter 163

But what is fairly well established – I continued sparklingly – is that (I put the cup down carefully on top of a folded newspaper, rather than on the perhaps valuable immediate surface of the table itself) – is, I repeat, that the earth's atmosphere some 3 to 4 thousand million years ago (I know I am not entirely precise, do forgive me) – did it not consist of, or largely of, methane and ammonia. Eh? Do you deny it? She looked at me in a slightly disenchanted way, dandling a child (her own daughter – and perhaps mine too!) on one or both of her delicious knees.

Chapter 164

And water vapour too, of course – I added almost at once. I looked round yet again. The garden was utterly empty. Considering that people have so undoubtedly been in them, and the voices occasionally so voluble or voracious, it is astonishing quite how empty such places can become. Someone was weeping remotely. A distant view of a water-influenced feature was not quite as I had remembered it being. I sighed and walked away, conscious that all creeds appear immortal even to their last believer. The birds continued what sounded like much the same absurd noise as before.

Chapter 165

Outside, however, the road was quiet. It was reaching out towards a bright, unimportant little town. This townlet was reaching equably towards its past, a period of equal contentment. Equal to what? To now, I suppose. The past reached out towards her hand (either will do; I forget which one) – which had recently reached out towards a remote-control switch. At that instant I could see her breasts, an event which always seems to me to be too important to be on the ordinary side of the end of creation. I was once again amazed as to why I had not stopped existing.

Chapter 166

Anyway, such, or a similar, was the conclusion I had come to. I do not vouch for its unerring accuracy. (She seems to think they are inadequate! One might as well suppose that a pair of universes are inadequate! But that is a poor comparison, for a pair of universes is surely impossible on strictly logical grounds, whereas breasts just seem impossible as a matter of fact.) I have not yet mentioned, I do not think, that the same old evening was urinating a rare golden light onto the top of my now unquestionably balding head. The nearby stairway, I safely assert, was very dark – even if only in the way that the molten sky can be very dark. No-one was walking up and down it. That is to say, no-one whom I could see. But the red carpet with yellow sinuosities in the corner of the room was for the moment an adequate and convincing substitute for them, whoever they are.

Chapter 167

Is my head really on at the proper angle, I asked her. Or perhaps I asked myself. Or she asked me. (No.) Or we asked each other. (No.) Or our non-existent children tried to ask, and so narrowly failed. Personally, I fear I begin to find these children tedious. Then a door opened sideways, and we saw an immense long view of a world painted inexpertly on top of a shimmering satiny surface of unnaturally brilliant colours.

Chapter 168

At such moments, moments such as this, the world seems unimprovable. Or perhaps it is simply that such a superfluous concept never occurs to us. Let me give another, almost equal example. Here we are, walking in a garden, near a lane and a half-demolished building which we never even knew was threatened. The light shines on us, and her clothes move. Let me stay here forever, just like this, is how I try to drag some of that silence into inadequate words. And yet, it, like everything else, is already changing – surely?

Chapter 169

No – it still seems to be the same. Am I already changing? Do not basely confuse me with so much distant noise – with so many whatever-it-ises of mass dissipated (I refer to that star there) whatever fraction it is of each microsecond. Why bother? This is someone who has torn photographs of stars out of unwanted, second-hand books, and has sheared off edges too extensive for a thousand million human lives to cross, so that it would fit on the wall between two photographs: a face of a world-famous dead man and a backside of an almost totally unknown living woman. I beg you not to force me to choose between them! I have also seen, on the steps outside the disappointingly small doorway to the nearest large library, blondes with ponytails and earrings, talking to men younger than me – a category of being the necessity of which has never yet seemed entirely convincing to me.

Well: *for the moment* they are younger than me. Let them enjoy it while they can. Some of them will be murdered.

Chapter 170

Perhaps I will be murdered too. I insist on changing the subject. Forgive me if I sink down under the earth, this beloved blessed earth which at times I value almost as the equal to one of the absolutely smallest hairs in your with a sigh he removes the word, not wishing to give offence, towards incomprehensibly violent (though my brother has recently acquired a book which contains some impressive pictures of the effects of volcanoes and earthquakes) granite and basalt – I do not guarantee the accuracy of these dauntingly technical terms – which is too packed with past footmarks to be impressed by the pressure of your sensible shoes (even though the thin pink lines on them are a nice idea). But I do not sink slowly through it like an unexpected subterranean sunrise, towards that floating area far below, almost weightless, where there is surely nothing but this garden, stretched out to a much wider extent, such as it deserves – this small, sloping garden made endless, made apparently endless. Far off, beaten against by waves neither calm nor killing, which serve to separate it from nothing but itself as it was yesterday, now a timeless distance away. I shall of course continue to take with me all this pressure on all my sensitive parts, including particularly my eyeballs, although I will leave behind us that tree, that tree, and, in particular, that tree too. Goodbye for ever.

Chapter 171

I have just remembered something else. It seems almost impossible to me now that there once was a morning when I took the opportunity to glance through the not quite fully closed door to my neighbour's garden, and discovered that he really was a bush, as I had seriously suspected all along. At once, a few dozen hitherto unfathomable events and mystifications became clear to me. Even though none of them struck me as being particularly important.

Chapter 172

But what I still did not understand was – why, whenever I sat down in a favourite nook of my own and attempted to imagine that I was a wall – a particular, interesting wall, containing an unpredictable feature like an apparently unnecessary corner or an old blocked-up threatening doorway – another man always appeared beside me, slightly drunk and slightly uninteresting. But why worry too much about such things? After all, none of us would exist at all if only our fathers had chosen not to ejaculate. What self-centred swines they all were, eh?

Chapter 173

Let me turn my head and consider more important things. This, for instance. Oh, the unbearable brilliance of flowers! Have I thrown away my youth like an unconsidered succession of cigarette packets – failing to check (it would not have been too difficult, would it? it would not have taken up much time) whether or not there are still any condom-like objects within them?

I fear so. So: who will pour a bucket of vibrating water over me tomorrow? No-one. Those days are surely gone now. Whereas today is, as usual, almost impossibly distant. Who now will scheme to swing open a furtive door for me, and allow me musical forbidden glimpses of possibly tiny females learning to dance, more or less, rather than turn into false coinage? Will you do it?

Chapter 174

Indulge these rambling reminiscences a moment further, I beg you. For I can still remember a time when I was too young to climb these stairs, or indeed these stars, unaided. Which of these blossoms – if only I knew! – would when plucked from their natural surroundings under or on the surface of the soil be able to learn to imitate or reciprocate or share my affection? Might someone not even learn to glory in it? Let her at least walk up and down beside or outside my window on a succession of summer days, content to be so regarded. All I need to do is to live and to die. But perhaps, not exactly among these houses. I feel there is a proper place somewhere else. Very near here, perhaps. But where?

Chapter 175

Where exactly am I at the moment anyway? I will tell you, whether or not you wish to know. I am standing at a window, reading.

My book rests on a small television set, which itself rests on the corner of a metal sink – an improvised lectern which I make much use of.

The Archduke's wife has just called out, "What has happened to you?" to her dying husband, and has fallen forward. The others in the car think she has merely fainted from shock.

"It is nothing", says the Archduke himself. He repeats that three times. He is dying too.

A click. Someone comes through the crimson door at the bottom of the garden. This is the garden which I am actually looking at.

An extremely elegant woman in black trousers, wearing a red blouse with black dots.

She walks slowly up the path, apparently thinking of something.

Chapter 176

I have a suspicion that she knows perfectly well that I am here, watching her. But, in the end, what is there matters much, except standing or being in rooms and gardens, not wishing to be elsewhere? Far off, the unseen little boundaries, where people in strange clothes and attitudes drift towards us and away from us. Only very rarely does anyone come leaping in through a window, in any sense of the term.

Chapter 177

What a morning! The houses hunch up their shoulders the better to receive its dazzling shock. One can tell, all the same, that they are taken aback by its unexpected enthusiasm. Water is absorbed in many places, both intentionally and unintentionally. The girls are in a small room with a boy who shrieks. For what is Fear but Hope in the nude?

Chapter 178

Not long afterwards, it is, as usual, morning. Down a long stairway rolls a particoloured head. Or ball. A child, presumably chastised, begins to cry at or near a window above us. As usual, no-one jumps out of it. Or, indeed, out of any of the numerous windows all around. How strangely well-behaved so many people are! What a superb world it would be, if only public standards of truth in discourse, particularly political discourse, would be set by the voice in which a decent, reasonable man talks to his wife's navel for almost an hour, thinking himself not overheard, in the darkness. Something colossal is falling down from the sky, but as it is only something which is always doing precisely that, no-one notices.

Chapter 179

(15 years pass, as usual.) We hear the sound of an unquestionably chastised child reverberating at an upper window. Yet, though it at once descends (as might be freely expected) towards the timid obedient ground, or perhaps the grass, or it may even be a cloud – nevertheless, just before it reaches the ground – a white cloth comes flying out of the same window! I saw something like that happen once. Who is doing this?

Chapter 180

But why do you ask? It is now dark – despite and not because of the incredible amount of windows all around us. I dread to think what might be happening at this somewhat criminal hour, at the top of that contiguous shaded stairway. And if I am at the top of that stairway? But, obviously, I am not. I am here. Whatever is hitting me softly on the head must be otherwise explained. Fortunately there is a more innocent, or at least a more legal, explanation, though never a believable one.

Chapter 181

(48,273 years pass, as usual.) Why then do I not know what is happening? Why will nobody help me? Where are all the advantageous women in the world, now that I need only one of them – or two of them at absolute most. Someone lounging in the next room gives a yawn of very pure boredom – I sense that infallibly. But perhaps one woman is always 17 too few, as St Ninian so typically put it. (I disagree, by the way.)

Chapter 182

It is, you will have noticed, almost evening. How an orange square of yesterday's light is picked out in the corner of the nearby building. I no longer need it. Do you? Cross your legs, if you wish, before you reply.

Chapter 183

Cars are travelling home typically in typically great numbers. Smashed cars, garaged cars, cars mysteriously defunct – these we do not see. Nor those of half a second ago. History rests equally on these cars and on women's eyelashes.

Chapter 184

Groups of people come out of doorways, usually less than four at a time, talking, usually less than five at a time. An easy trick, but one which I find I rather like. Their tones of voice let us know – except that we died so long before this – that tomorrow cannot possibly not arrive, and that talk about death is grotesquely exaggerated. I know they are wrong, although, of course, I agree with them. This is what comes of mixing two disparate sources. I expect their own views are, in reality, much the same.

Chapter 185

But enough of this evening, relatively pleasant though it may have been. In particular, I speak of that enjoyable period of crossing a bridge when, by the adroit positioning of my head (it was utterly necessary to look a little backwards), I saw the brightness of the almost full moon negotiate a sequence of long thin puddles, between dead leaves and abandoned empty cigarette cartons – more probably the result of some miscalculation by the unseen builders than (I mean the declivity, the line of depression) than than than an endless wearing-out by passing footsteps. Later, I slip down the flickeringly lit corridor and into the most promising room in the building. Once there, I close the door behind me.

I am a little disappointed that it was not locked, for I have unofficially acquired keys to all the doors in this house.

Chapter 186

In fact, now that I remember, it *was* locked. She will not be back for an hour or two. I do not mean a century or two, despite this throbbing in or near my heart. If I remember rightly, her spell of dutiful activity will not end until thirty minutes before midnight.

Oh yes, let her continue to work in her little office, sending out messages all over the world – actually, I am not too sure what it is her job entails, but no matter, no matter. What is important is that I am here and she is not. A pleasant reversal of the usual state of affairs. Pleasant, and yet somehow also undeniably tragic.

Chapter 187

I remove my clothes with a tiresome lack of calmness, and place them inside the large fur-lined pouch which this time I have not neglected to bring with me. Her own small imitation-fur jacket is hanging near the door. I cross to it and manoeuvre my way into it as best I can.

I note that a letter lies on a fragile, tremulous table near the bed. I read through it expertly and am disappointed by its jejune tone. Perhaps it was not really she who wrote it, but a crude facsimile of her who finds me genuinely uninteresting.

Chapter 188

Next, as the hair or fur begins to sprout ever more luxuriously on my body, I look round for any screaming little bowl or box or other such palpitating receptacle wherein she deposits her so enviably fortunate earrings.

These I soon locate, lying idly beside a cupboard, all still bearing signs of obvious resentment at their abrupt dismissal from one or two of the loveliest extremities of her body. Caressingly, I pick up as many of them as possible in these sadly gnarled paws, and bow my grossly expanded head over in order to inspect them fondly. Do any of them, I wonder, as yet show signs of damage from the ferocity of my previous attentions?

Chapter 189

Yes. This one here, an intricate bifurcated fernlike shape, is perhaps beginning to seem a little frayed. I give it several dozen kisses, over half of them passionate, and replace it with all the care these untended claws can manage in as nearly as possible the position in which I found it. Another one I quickly take into a cupboard with me – a more robust design, clearly, to my eye, based on a system near to or like the Crab Nebula. Come with me, my proud beauty!

Chapter 190

So engrossed am I in my exalted enterprise – and one vitally necessary too, of course, for the continuance of my species – that I do not at first hear the door open, five or so seconds later – let us call it 13 minutes – when she comes into the room, following a treacherous new timetable which has been horrifyingly operative since the previous Thursday.

Perhaps she was alerted by noticing the cataclysm in her cupboard suddenly stop. Knowing that she was there awoke in me – I will not seek an undeserved reputation for *savoir faire* by denying it – a moment of deep unease. After all, women (any seven of whom are identical, save only for their innumerable differences) are notoriously predictable, and frequently emotionally immature. There are, I regret to say, many of whom it could truthfully be said that to open a cupboard, thereby more surprisingly than not discovering a nude next-door neighbour attempting to unite with the missing one of a pair of ornamental earrings would be very likely to bring out the worst and least reasonable aspects of their psyche. However, one does not like to be too harsh. Let me reserve my own opinion on this one. For she, for instance, when she opened the cupboard door, merely remarked, "Ah! So that's where she's got to!", and, reaching in, perhaps wondering how it could possibly have got there, which under the circumstances showed, or so I thought, an imperceptiveness verging on the cruel –.

Chapter 191

It was just here that, with a single gesture of irritation, I intercepted his irritating and quite possibly (however superficially convincing it might have been) mendacious narrative. After all, it was not *him* whom I wished to listen to. It was *her*. True, it would be accurate to say that she was no longer there, but a particularly strong memory had nonetheless overwhelmed me.

So I tore out his heart, and then flung it up to some birds that were passing, which devoured it without thanking me for sustenance in their unending flight. Next, I fitted an accurate, keen mirror above certain recent disturbing events in my mind. However, no matter how assiduously I attempted to concentrate, I could not even begin to think why I should so suddenly (a word I love using) have remembered that moment (a word

I love using), which I had otherwise or hitherto forgotten for my entire life.

It is peculiar, is it not, that it should have lain unused in an unvisited attic of my head for so long. Let me extend this object now.

Chapter 192

I was reposing on my back in a small bed, even though I did not think I was Leonardo da Vinci (but then, at such an age, neither did *he* think that), and my mother was standing close beside me, doing something fairly essential, as usual. Not far away, my small sister was – no, it's no use: I can't remember that. What was she doing? Why did she have to have her legs so baroquely parted while she was doing it? Was she washing her feet? Clipping her toenails? Showing up the inadequacies and rigidities of the architecure?

And what was I doing? Yes, I was investigating the ceiling far above me.

Chapter 193

All at once, I became aware of a terrific, perhaps preternatural power flooding through me, and I stepped up and called to my mother and sister by name. I knew both their names. Even so, they seemed not to hear me. They carried on doing whatever it was they had been doing before I had opened my mother (mouth, surely?) and thrown surely adequate vocables at them. I glimpsed the possibility that a thinking woman is a normal physical event.

Chapter 194

I also realized then that I was in a world (or a room – I did not quite make that distinction at that time) (it is still not an easy one to make) which contained both a female whose already active genitalia had produced *me* – as well, it appeared, as various other objects – and which also contained at the same time another female, whose head was usually less near to the ceiling, and who teased me by briefly flaunting, then primly hiding, then showing me again almost as briefly, and so forth, her own version of a fascinating physical detail whose purpose one was entirely unable even to guess at at bath-time. This had a perhaps not wholly predictable effect on me.

Chapter 195

A huge wind – why should I not now call it a gale? – blew through me and I rustled all my leaves, more to indicate my mere presence than anything else. I crackled my foliage, swayed my branches, and, to be perfectly honest, raged. At times a snowstorm even swept by me, which I ignored.

Chapter 196

Nonetheless, it was strange to see the two females going on about their business as if nothing had happened, even while covered with light heaps of snow, moving about in a world which was by now thoroughly dusted with the stuff.

Chapter 197

Eventually, they swept up all the snow, using little brushes and scoops. Then, sometimes one after the other, sometimes together, sometimes years apart, they carried it out into the yard and released it as if accidentally into the air. Needless to say, the vagina of the sky was as usual uninterested in the worn suffering roofs of the habitations of humans, below which speech was being poured out, heat was being poured out, the possibilities necessary for human beings were being poured out, as were more minutes, more minutes, more minutes, seeping through the usual apertures; so that, bored, it turned for solace to a godlike celestial penis, capable (after the fashion of such celestial objects) of understanding it, and thus a heavenly banging sounded just above the roofs all night.

Chapter 198

And perhaps that explains some of the sounds which I am continually hearing. Even if I do not exactly hear them, that is not the most important thing. The most important thing, surely, is that such sounds are always being made. That is to say: things are happening which our ears would interpret as noises, were our ears there, which, of course, they are not. Strictly speaking, they rarely are. Our ears are more or less absent from everywhere.

Chapter 199

Moreover we can hardly justly claim that sight is different, despite the fact that I am extremely fortunate in being able to vary at will the rate at which I see things.

I never cease to be grateful towards the being whom I consider to be responsible for this and for other disasters, even should this not be the secretive daughter of a neighbour, who is gazing through her father's superb extended telescope, while she absent-mindedly scratches a sexual object which is not her delightful head.

Chapter 200

Thus, I casually look across a room, and the deep brownish eyes which I wish to see return their gaze at me for an immense number of years, while the occasional rain falls so slowly that each drop is a stopped pebble sinking or slipping down the sky, all of its motion unobservable. Beauty is beauty, but pebbles are small stones, usually less in size than a rock, or even a planet.

Chapter 201

Her pronunciation of a single word – let us say "I" – is a race of amazing animals slowly developing and slowly disappearing, after having, to the astonishment of the brutal interstellar dust, after having reached the unprecedented stage of culture revealed when one is able to sit down and absent-mindedly scratch an indescribably adorable sexual object (a phrase which I still love using).

Chapter 202

Or, irritably, I rub my eyes – my brown eyes the colour of a particularly rare and joyful sky – and human beings have arrived and have utterly departed before I am even able to spit out into a plastic bag near the window, on this morning of the last day of the sixth month of the 89th year of the century, intended for rubbish, some infringement of mucus which I assume, for all I know, has accumulated in my throat or thereabouts during the latest unmemorable night. So. I have spat the mucus towards the bag.

I doubt if any American would ever say that. How long ago was it, or any of it, part of a star? Or any of this? Light hurries across the garden outside. A balloon tethered to a washing-pole yesterday evening still hangs there this morning. Dots appear in the air. Rain??

Chapter 203

So: what shall I do today? Am I still in love? Or has that not yet changed into something else too? A pair of beating wings is or are somewhere very near me.

Chapter 204

But I have learned, I think, that it is useless to turn round quickly, in the hope of discerning their exact position. Such at least is my personal view of the situation. Or of evolution.

Chapter 205

I trust that mere non-existence would not disqualify one from having a view on such a vital subject. Or perhaps I am being over-dramatic in claiming that I do not exist. (But did I ever make such a claim?)

Perhaps I nearly exist. Or perhaps I am nearly or merely asleep.

In which case, I perhaps have more answers than questions.

Chapter 206

In which case, let me suppose that a telescope falling from a tree hit me on the head and awakened me from my midday nap. I looked at the joyous figures milling all around me in the walled garden, and it struck me with a rare force that I was the father of 2 sons and 3 daughters. What extraordinary ideas arithmetic can get itself involved with! Truly, I am amazed that this is the sort of thing which it is ever possible to forget. And how many do you think have forgotten such things by now? Guess by all means. No-one can genuinely guess a high enough number.

Chapter 207

Certainly, I must stop my illicit intrigues with actresses. I can see now that my preferred rationalization of this – that I am merely doing so in order to gather adequate quantities of pubic hair, sufficient for presentation to a Higher Institution of Learning (preferably one concerning itself with History – although Technology will do at a pinch, for I have been forced to use a wide variety of scissors) – this sort of excuse now seems shabby and evasive to me. I must lead a better life. Which is to say, I must try to make a better job of leading the same one. Ah, how wonderful it was to hear the children shriek when I could easily have been dead during my latest snooze. I looked at them lovingly, and tried to foretell their futures. Then I attempted to get out of my chair.

I have succeeded in doing this sort of thing often enough before. Nonetheless, this time I experienced a strange difficulty in doing so. I tried and failed severally. Meanwhile the children continued their games. Ignorant and ungrateful little turds! Could they, hypnotized by so much energy, not even suspect what disaster was happening to me?

Chapter 208

I slumped back, exhausted. By now I am thoroughly exhausted. There was also a distressing heat in the sun, which I felt was making a sarcastic foreign point about the unnecessity of my presence in the venue. I confess I thought this showed rather bad taste. I was hurt. I was distinctly miffed.

So I picked up a few years in my free left hand, and threw them towards the happy others, seeking to catch their attention.

Chapter 209

I failed.

Chapter 210

So, allow me fifty or so years earlier to lean my head back further. A little further. It is not inconveniencing you, I take it – is it? And still a little further if I may. Which reminds me. Is she still there? Is she still there at the bottom of the garden, pretending not to be aware that I have observed her?

What does it matter?

Perhaps I have genuinely failed to observe her.

Chapter 211

This beverage, prompted from who now knows quite what Highland burn, in which loveletters have urinated and sheep disappeared (that should really be vice-versa, but I am in a flippant mood), meteorites splashed, drunks fallen, abandoned shoes swept hurriedly past – and look at that gloomy army hurrying morosely through it!

I will now and for the rest of my life give my full attention to this beverage and to such beverages as these. (The author is teetotal, by the way.)

Chapter 212

Of course, it no longer tastes the same now that she no longer complains about my overuse of it.

Chapter 213

But what warmth in my throat nonetheless! And on it goes, onwards ever onwards, down into the unseen ornate caverns of my interior, through which one surgeon and various displaced women wander, weeping bemusedly to themselves in foreign languages.

Such mornings as this! Such sunlight as if destined from the beginning of the world, which we know it never was.

On days like this, various of the women in the interior of my intestines happen to meet, try haltingly to converse, and then, in their mutual excitement – oh, excuse me – but I feel such a moment of internal calm as I walk down a sunlit busy road, confident that at least for now, for now, for now, the existence of this world, even if it does not truly exist, yet cannot be disproved. Oh, you! You whose far too perfect voice – I have far too often fallen asleep while still trying to conjure it up accurately. Shall I ever hear you smile again? Yes; I truly suppose I shall. But let it be soon. Let it be soon, for that is a silver hair fastened round the thumbtack which secures your picture to a wall in the room where I sleep or, more often, fail to sleep.

Chapter 214

What will happen? Later, a window will open in a light-filled wall.

Later, I will see several other windows below, still in the darkness.

Later, as I turn my head to depart, I will realize with a start that I have been given an invitation to return, even though only as the same person.

There will even be the sounds of children nearby, as usual.

Chapter 215

Other people, other people, other people. But, for now, the cool paradisial garden is quiet and yet perfectly appointed. The elaborate, voluminous chairs, scattered to take account of the many sights worth seeing, are mostly unsat-in. Or unsatin. Or unsat-on. The occasional leaf, being as noisy as it can be, is blown in irregular gusts across the lawn.

Why do we suppose that contentment itself is always about to provoke a vengeful reaction?

Chapter 216

Why can we never quite forget that there is a figure flitting somewhere among the trees and houses, sniggering every so often, and reminding us in general that we are not in control? Must we pass through door after door after door, only for this? Must, as Thomson would surely have put it, Nature struggle against Illness, only to be told by Existence (its inefficient doctor) that Death or Something Worse is waiting, Pregnant, at the foot of a Narrow Stairway? What do you think?

Chapter 217

Why may we not live ourselves in the air, as viruses intermittently live in the bloodstream of the beloved, thought happy, but in this guise without the power to hurt or be hurt?

Chapter 218

Why, when a sleeping girl shakes her head, do we not also feel our own heads being shaken?

Chapter 219

Sometimes we do, I suppose.

Chapter 220

In fact, sometimes we feel our entire selves being shaken.

Chapter 221

Why, that is to say, are we too big to slip behind people's eyes anyway, given that we can love their perfectly feasible eyes so much?

Chapter 222

On the other hand, why, whenever we lose a serious game is it necessary that the unused genitalia of our favourite disciples should appear teasingly together in the corner of our eye, making it seem for a moment (deceitfully of course) as if everything is about to be either covered in a single striped green sheet or understood?

I ask these questions only because I must. That should be obvious.

Chapter 223

Actually, that is a shameless lie. In fact, much of this consists of straightforward uninteresting lies, although needless to say I have not seen fit to draw direct attention to this aspect of my thrusting investigation. Let us rather turn our view to the beautiful world all around us, now that the afternoon sits bright and prim on the lawn, reluctant to move for fear that people leap to the conclusion that it is drunk.

Chapter 224

Women are walking through the streets nonetheless. Surely it is not that they fear nothing. Most things are in hiding. Oh, perhaps there is something in Stevenson's dictum that every woman has been fitted with at least one aperture which properly belongs to quite another female, but I cannot believe that that, even if it were true, would be true. But that is a very dangerous sort of remark to make, I'm sure you'll agree, for one should not be flippant about the truth.

Chapter 225

Let us instead hit time over the head with that large, flat instrument which is lying near the doorway. A table? Six months? A single telephone call? A photographic postcard?

However, we can be sure that the disappearing bird, though it may start to sing, will never fly again. Yet I am careful to let none of this prevent me from picking the glass up.

Chapter 226

So I picked the glass up from the table and sniffed it carefully. Its contents, I feared, did not have the texture of normal apple-juice.

Had my beloved, if such she still was, in a fit of absent-mindedness poured out the wrong liquid entirely, before going off into the distant corner behind the cooker to reproduce asexually?

A brief explosion occurred, as it will. Perhaps the result of electrical discharges, shock waves, past arguments, or ultra-violet radiation (which comes from the sun). I raised an eyebrow in surprise, and walked unsteadily across the room.

You appear – I said to her with some asperity – to have given me the theoretical origin of life, rather than just nice everyday ordinary buy-here-at-a-cheaper-price apple-juice. Look! Organic molecules of considerable complexity have been accidentally formed! What do you say to that?

Chapter 227

That is hardly my fault, she replied, and indicated her dissatisfaction by clapping her hands together – thereby crushing the animal which had hubristically thought to fly roughly between them.

I reflected. Perhaps I should drink it anyway, I remarked – even though it does not look like the last thoughts of anyone called Ramsay to me. Nor, may I add, the accidental discovery of (I think) Neptune by (I think) Galileo who, even though it was visibly moving, nonetheless unthoughtfully interpreted the mark as a star.

A door slammed nearby. Our neighbour was (I think) going out to work. What does he do all day I wonder.

Chapter 228

An alert insect would or could have clambered up from the liquid and waited at the rim of the glass, had I not already drunk the contents a moment before. Ha! Another modest victory for the mammalia!

You ought not to have done that, she said. Now not even the least weed (how charmingly her lips trembled) in the sea will ever develop on this planet. Yes: this planet here. How can you do such things? I'm tired of you. You think of no-one all the time but yourself.

Her shoulders slumped and she sat down disgracefully. I sometimes think it was a great mistake of mine to reply to that ridiculous phonecall you made a year ago next month.

Chapter 229

A shy cryptocleidus – perhaps the animal known only from relics of its footprints? – looked in at the window from outside, smiling. Presumably it had formed its long tail into an archway so that the numerous cars could continue to pass. Satisfied at what it saw, it moved away.

Chapter 230

But a cryptocleidus is a marine dinosaur, she objected pettishly. How could it have got here? After all, the street has a subdued hidden entrance, and the view from here is not particularly pleasant – certainly not, I shouldn't think, for something so long extinct.

Also, I do not see any of its footprints among the parked cars, or the moist tyremarks of their contemporaries.

Chapter 231

Yes, yes, my dear. Yes, I added. Anything you say. I am a cretin and you are Madame Curie. (For I know better than to provoke an argument with her.) All the same – I would not have objected to life occurring. Nor, I suspect, would she. Nor would the fly which flew unharmed past the space where one of us should have been.

Chapter 232

As I say, no-one or nothing would have objected. However, I settled instead for the simpler, more cowardly course and merely changed the subject. I prefer to leave it a fairly open question as to whether or not I am still lying. I replaced my head on my shoulders at the proper angle and asked her the following question: what are you reading and how many people are in that cupboard?

Chapter 233

Really! What a reaction! There are some women who seem to think – merely because you have, as much out of kindness and respect towards them as anything else – or perhaps even motivated entirely by boredom – fed at their more obvious sources of nourishment, that they can tell significant lies to you, whether it is raining outside or inside the room or not, and that you must either believe them or pretend to do so. But what they forget is that when the core of a fruit is thrown out of the window, the room will not then pipe up and suggest that the anus of the previous occupant of that small chair is strikingly like a mirror in a beautiful field, regretted by all those who would have been willing to shed blood in the noble cause of freedom (and who perhaps did), which is perhaps the only truly noble cause. Now someone wheezes in the sunlight, on the far side of an inoperative canal. Will it? The window swings back, and sunlight or the fruit is thrown in again. So it goes on for a few of the best few afternoons of an entire life.

Chapter 234

For instance, take the next one. I am seated on this chair. I am wondering how so much blue sky can possibly have got into the room, when only we two are present.

She is seated on that chair. No-one will ever succeed in producing such a wine. As, for instance, her presence. As, for instance, her hair. As, for instance, the pattern of tiny marks on her cheek and neck, some too perfect musical notation just beyond audibility.

Chapter 235

No-one is seated on the third chair. The easily available music continues to play.

And no-one is seated on a fourth chair either. This flight of sardonically smiling minutes passing continually through the air.

Chapter 236

But who is that in the fifth chair?

Chapter 237

Or who has taken away a fifth chair?

Chapter 238

But one thing is always missing, and there is always too the nagging doubt that it is not properly preserved somewhere else, perhaps because immortal beings are incapable of appreciating it at its full value. (Immortal beings, of course, are a metaphor for anything numinous which has to do with her eyes, however vaguely. I mean other things as well, of course, but I am reluctant to keep mentioning the same parts of her body. I should have paid more attention years ago to the vocabulary of anatomy.)

Chapter 239

Yet, I expect I will mutate soon enough into an entity which eats clouds. After all, clouds too pass through these our rooms, do they not? Sometimes they even slowly shape into the form of particularly disliked teachers. Sometimes they are gas particles seeking a world of intelligence. So many words; so many arguments.

Do the people who were here before us still exist? Are they as lost as a violent verbal disagreement on a keen morning 16 years ago (how appalling I was at that age – I blush to think about it) – or, which would surely be even worse, on a sunlit golden evening 616 years ago? Look away quickly by all means!

Chapter 240

Perhaps to these many lines of liquid shattering against each other in walled valleys. All for what? A few words trickle to earth like the last drops of rain. The past is a previous cloud-formation. Even so, the storm is long since by. A few hours later, no-one even knew that it existed. This is perhaps a slight exaggeration, which perhaps tends to disqualify it from being an accurate image for the existence and durability of the human race. So what?

Chapter 241

Gradually now, other things begin to learn other things. What else is one to expect from history? To the rocks, death is equally trivial. Am I a storm? Are you a moment's calmness? Are you these clouds which are listening to me? And is this one my laughter? The world divides up into male and female like a mouth realizing that it has an upper and a lower jaw.

Jaws begin to chew the air. Yet what can they spit out at the end, I wonder, but the unwanted unremarkable bones of us or of huge fish or of tiny creatures which may even indeed have been exceptionally intelligent? Of course they are more intelligent than the air, but where we can derive surer limits is not clear to everyone.

They will certainly not spit out any desire for a moment of happiness glimpsed at this window to be infinitely prolonged, and not merely because such a concept is a contradiction in terms. No; such objects will not disturb the otherwise featureless ground.

Or air, or space, or flat endless stretch of water. But any moment shorter than infinity is threatened with insufficiency even by your half-smile. But your half-smile can only rise in a world without such an infinity, perhaps while I struggle with a difficult lock.

Chapter 242

This inevitably (a word I detest using, except when I am lying) leads to an exchange of a few more words beside a cooling gas-fire.

One of us has a large thin metal utensil held in the hand.

Who is hoping for anything to change significantly?

Yet again, a breeze does not knock the wall down.

Nor that wall, with a picture on it of an actress who reminds me of you.

And, as if to set the climax on our joy, a plane does not fall through the roof, full of our anguished sharpened hopes.

Chapter 243

A chair stands motionless for hour after hour.

Chapter 244

Upstairs, someone, at least one person, is lying on a bed but is not asleep.

Chapter 245

Can anyone possibly really have died? More than one person?

Chapter 246

After all, if we did not belong here, we would not be here at all, would we – not at the start and not at the finish.

Chapter 247

And not at any point in between either.

Chapter 248

Could we really not fit them all, all of them, into this small room?

Chapter 249

Elsewhere, such a gas-fire is still burning.

Chapter 250

And in the morning more sunlight.

In the morning, nearby, a definite sound of someone singing.

Soft objects are walking through the sunlight everywhere. This causes me to regret that I do not visit the real ground more often than I do.

Chapter 251

Nature, however, produces philosophers and cucumbers without *parti pris*. I wonder sometimes whether or not the light really does change as much as I think it does. Once, I think I could have stood still for entire hours, letting the known world rearrange itself in whichever way it liked around me. It would have done much the same anyway. Then off I started on a journey to school or to some other supposed institution of learning. Meanwhile, at home, our mothers do mysterious things, until, quite suddenly (a word which I have used before), we return and are allowed to see them again several hours later.

/

Chapter 252

When a child eats a meal, it does not think of battles at the other end of a tunnel of earth, does it? It does not feel itself to be within a pair of nets, quite unlike thighs, from which it cannot shake itself free. It may sometimes suspect that it is a naked woman past which, or out of which, a noble river, scarcely navigable (almost a lake), is flowing, but, frankly, I very much doubt it. After all, day and night are changing places obsessively across the river.

Chapter 253

What does it matter to us? I am incoherent after such a night. It is always morning on this side of the river. That is why I have chosen to live here. We are putting food into our mouths, as usual. That is to say: extinct sunrises, sudden growth in children, a sense of security, a small flame burning where it ought not to be – or any other such vegetable which one of us at least actually detests but keeps quiet about. For who can tell with certainty whether it is better to keep his spiritual vagina open or closed? Move! Move again! But not towards the window.

Chapter 254

When a falling feather turns in the sky we are now on the other side of the river ourselves. What darkness there is in this room, apart from one area, beside a corner, ludicrously flooded by the sun. Is it possible to believe that this room is ever bare, nude, lifeless, unoccupied? It is difficult to be sure, particularly given that there are so many beetles on this benighted planet.

Chapter 255

Yet I suspect that it is not I, or only I, who am present, but a woman bravely struggling with tears. Do you not believe that I will phone you as soon as I plausibly can? It is not possible that we are an identical person, whatever my first notion of this sentence might have been. Oh, Possibility! What a goddess she must be. I suppose she must have at least five of everything. A lovely possibility, perhaps, though so much depends on one's mood.

Chapter 256

But more lovely than that, and certainly more lovely than the doubtless extremely low chance formation of a membraneous coating surrounding one of the very earliest terrestrial cells or cell-like structures (ah! that melodious phrase again!), her tousled head emerged through the arcs of the reticulated bed-cover, piquant as happening to meet two Swedes early on a damp evening, and directing them towards a difficult-to-find building (the Youth Hostel of course) on top of a fine nearby hill. But, needless to say, far more attractive.

Good morning, she said – an almost impossible event!

After all, five seconds before her conception she did not exist. There was no form in which she was existing. And five seconds afterwards, she was incapable of recording her own voice on a cassette-player. Five months afterwards, she could not argue about either the psychology of time or the pros and cons of abortion. Need I add that she was not aborted?

Five years afterwards, she could not tell you the capital of China; five decades afterwards she (of course) could not understand what was going on inside her eldest child's mind; five centuries afterwards, she could not listen to her own voice on a cassette-recorder. But I insist on saying that I will nevertheless not forget that adorable voice.

Chapter 257

For instance, when she said to me that the main problem is that we somehow think that the past is piling up behind us; rather in the nature of libraries of history-books; that it is all falling into a large box somewhere, out of which we will be able to pull it, or any single part of it, whenever we want to. This is a mistake.

Chapter 258

It was also a mistake of mine to contort my face into a disgusting leer as if it were at all appropriate to anything she had just observed. But we all have our endearing little traits, most of which drive our loved ones berserk, usually with anger.

And do you perhaps think it is more like something else, I asked her, with the understanding smile of one who realises that every cell in his body is clearly different from every other one.

Chapter 259

It is simply what happens in the spaces between things that are different, she replied. Or rather, that are difference. It is, I suppose, the spaces themselves. Or the spaces are what are different. That is to say, I suppose, it is an arrangement between other things, mistaken for a thing itself. No differences, no spaces, no time. (Intended as both a temporal and a logical sequence.)

Chapter 260

Perhaps it could best be explained as a sort of cleavage, she remarked, reaching back to adjust her bra.

Chapter 261

So, to talk of time on its own, I asked pensively, thereby (alas) drifting ever more inexorably towards mere fiction, is like talking of cleavage divorced from breasts, is it? I found this deeply convincing, for I have always regarded a woman putting on a bra as being an interesting – nay, fascinating – lesson in cosmology. And just as Fame – or, indeed, History in general – can be civilized and utterly charming, so of course (far more inevitably so) is a bra draped over the back of a chair not far from a radio, whether it is playing music or not. What dreadful lives the tone-deaf must have led before that vestment's invention! We must assume, however, as good rationalists, that it is the radio which is actually emitting the music, even though we are likewise committed to the truth of Carlyle's aperçu that to be fully human is to be obsessed by little tits. Some have questioned the word 'little', but I have thought it better to give the utterance as he actually formulated it. When the music stops, what appalling news will we hear – of deaths and threatened deaths, no doubt, and not a word about the at times terrifying friendliness of cleavage. And yet, how wonderful music seems, while one can forget female eyebrows!

Chapter 262

But she was looking at me as if I were already a different person entirely. I grew thoughtful and silent. The person whom I almost was, or who almost was me (neither term is entirely accurate – or, indeed, accurate at all) did not entirely exist, and therefore did not sit in my seat, looking out of the window, worried. As for myself, I was slightly worried.

Chapter 263

After all, how long has she been there for, I wondered, working away writing something in the falling or failing light?

Oh, we know all the old fears about such light never returning.

Life, eh? So much suffering – to turn into a sharp downpour, through which cars continue to spray past.

Are we not in one of these cars?

Chapter 264

Are we perhaps in one of the next cars?

Chapter 265

Looking at the lines cast idly by the sun, we suspect we are on the wrong planet entirely.

Chapter 266

But not on this one, perhaps, where there are basins and bowls of water scattered apparently at random over the floor. Why do the windows open and shut haphazardly? Why is there darkness beyond? No – now there is light. (After all, if women are moonlight, men are moonlight too.) But why?

The surface of the bowls of water shiver. As if, though the bowls are many, the surface is only one. It is said that at times all the surfaces will shiver independently (like life), but, speaking for myself, I have never seen this happen. I have, however, heard them sing out together a unison note which nothing in existence previous had prepared me for, except a fortunate voice or two.

Even in a foreign city the vessels sing, the vessels sing.

Chapter 267

Are we yet tired of wakening up in the morning? Let us throw clothes towards ourselves anyway. Even if they miss, they do not at once float on in or into interstellar space; or fill in a neat gasp in history between the disappearance of icosahedral semi-transparent fishes which thrive electronically, and the existence of those odd creatures capable of inventing such bizarre life-forms – or should I say, descriptions of such bizarre forms – or should I say, ourselves. As if you and I were a similar form of life. Are we? Are we not?

Chapter 268

I have thought of something else. Are we only a similar form of life but not quite? Disregard the sad fact that it is morning, and that therefore women are talking to each other in the street.

Other roads are of course being built.

Other roads are being finally closed. How many of us are inside these houses?

Chapter 269

How many of us, for instance, know where she is going?

Chapter 270

Now the street is empty. Look: you can see it is empty, can't you?

Chapter 271

But here – look! – is a picture of the same street later in the day. Now it is empty again, but in another way. That is to say, it is as empty as my awareness of having once been a few leaves – almost a full waving branch, apparently! – which the beak or mouth or claws of an animal whose sighing extinction a long time later was never followed by anyone or anything else ever giving a momentary thought about any single example of this species, tore brusquely out of their natural space to feed on them. After all, it had to feed somehow. Perhaps it even enjoyed them.

Chapter 272

Let us not be egocentric. Let us not injure each other too much. I mean to say, we are all extinct species, if time is as big as we have reason to believe it might be.

Chapter 273

Let us not, my darling, mistake our letters for stars. Not even for interplanetary messengers. (Whether we actually sent them, or merely thought of doing so.)

Chapter 274

Let us not behave like sunlight; not even as a sexualized sunlight. Perhaps everything is happening in the next space. Perhaps nothing in the one after it. I do not know.

Chapter 275

Well. I have seen beauty. I have seen sunlight. I have also seen how normal a vast other life is. I have heard a voice whispering not very far away from me.

Chapter 276

It may be possible that no-one has really loved me, but I have looked into many windows, and I have caught intentional glances which I hope I was not duped by.

I have even glimpsed music taking on shape before my eyes. After all, all music aspires to the condition of music, just as surely as all literature aspires to the condition of women's navels.

Chapter 277

I have perhaps watched it deliberately walk away from me, and I was never quite able to believe that it would not return. Or perhaps it did return later, and I myself was not there.

Chapter 278

But it would be pointless to regret that we are only mirror images of what we should be. Or to suppose that our happiness must always be one day in advance of us all.

Chapter 279

Yet I have always had the keen suspicion throughout my life that I was the hidden person sleeping on the other side of a locked door. Of course, I often wake up – but frequently only because of the noise which someone leaving makes in slamming it shut.

Chapter 280

But why? Have I been given vitally important treasures to guard? If so, why?

Chapter 281

If I remember rightly, I did not ask to be given them.

Chapter 282

Enough of this. Through that window I can see a famous scholastic building. Through that other window, the moon. From one of them occasionally drifts the sound of singing.

Chapter 283

Why then do I so like the sight of small rooms unengulfed in flames? Is it because I have heard too many doors close? Is it as simple as that?

Chapter 284

But in the morning I went over to the wall beside the door and found there two identical coats – where I had left only one the night before. So, she has disappeared, has she? Can it be possible? I suppose it is irrational to fear that if women were 11% more terrifying, the very continuation of the species would be threatened.

Chapter 285

I am surprised that I, or whoever this person is who so more than intermittently occupies the space where I am, should allow myself to be devastated more than once by the extent to which the opposite sex, whichever it is, should be capable of deceit. After all, unlike J.C. Maxwell, I do not believe that every woman is at heart a 13-amp fuse.

Chapter 286

Nor should I forget how capable of deceit I am myself. (Nor, needless to say, should you.)

Chapter 287

All the same, I cannot help thinking that their disconcerting female habit of changing into avenues into a golden, shimmering distance should have alerted me to their essential nature long ago. Yet I suspect that if they had had an essential nature, I would have noticed it, for that is the sort of incoherence which I have tried to train myself to notice that it is impossible to notice. But hear this: men and women are not finalists, whether opposing or not, in some vast cosmic game. Nor are they – whatever appearances might suggest to the contrary – wearing team strips.

Chapter 288

Later on in the morning, I looked through the bedding with exquisite care, but I could find no trace of her.

Chapter 289

Then a sort of net or fabric or cloth fell on top of me, hampering my movements, and rendering me temporarily helpless and blind. I heard the distinctive sound of a door opening and a column of imaginary giggling women (but not more than five of them) running out of the room one after the other. Ah! These magical series of connected sounds! Can it have been so long since last I heard them? Given the existence of such voices, what music should be possible!

Chapter 290

Then I slept soundly for the rest of the morning, while elsewhere in the city people died – or perhaps were born – in considerable numbers and not quite in the same way. Oh, granted, it is better to die in someone else's bed than in your own, but why should a brain not come into existence much as it degenerates – much like clouds, in fact?

Chapter 291

After all, the clouds of the morning are never sick, are they?

They might lower in the sky like the brooding pain in someone's head, but that someone is never quite visible. The ill shiver in bed. Occasionally other rather bored people deign to glance at them.

Chapter 292

Or distraught people gaze at them with expressions of white taut tension, as distorted as an edited recording of the first day of the year. Or as reassuring as a sparkling glass of undrunk medicine. Or as forgotten as the last sigh of a dead aunt's dead neighbour's dead grandmother. Or as cruel as a perfectly ordinary world containing nothing more intelligent than choreographed grass.

Then they go away, weeping.

Chapter 293

The next day, somehow, is normal. All is impossibly bright and usual. Our adolescent relatives begin, not nearly at exactly the same moment, to masturbate. At each of those moments an army surrenders.

Chapter 294

Time or War, or the average between the two, batters at the walls, and the forgetful occupant coughs slightly. After all, we are invariably surrounded by rooms which we never enter. Someone is snoring in most of them. Bright lights have shone in all of them. Darkness and a bird flying through it is all that is left of some. Plates smash. Lives smash. Planets smash. Hopes smash. But rocks reform, after a while, or after another while.

Chapter 295

It is certainly not such a consideration which reminds me of how often I (or whoever it was used to occupy much the same space) used to sleep in a bed set in an alcove in a wall.

Chapter 296

In the morning, I would walk through the curtain of my improvised little room, and what sunlight would be waiting for me in the larger room beyond!

Chapter 297

Even then I keenly felt an awkward sense of loss among so much gain: to think that I could only unquestionably waken up once a day, and only once be introduced to that light!

Chapter 298

Sometimes there were animals waiting for me in the next room!

Chapter 299

Later on – though, alas, I now see that it was never often enough – I would have to remove a young woman from the top of my head before going out in the morning.

Chapter 300

It was, of course, the stomach of my mother which first made me deeply happy. If I had been honest, I would have mentioned that before. And what am I to say of various other women?

Chapter 301

Truly, on the day when entirely by my own efforts I liberated the whole country from tyranny and established a type of society and a mode of government which enlightened unprejudiced judges everywhere hail as one of the greatest successes of our time – I could go further now but modesty precludes such a course of action – I must be honest with you. What was I doing? I was mentally comparing my feelings with those I had when I used to appear from behind that bed-alcove curtain every morning – except on the few occasions (perhaps after a break-in) when I was sleeping elsewhere, and my conclusions – well, I need not be too explicit about my conclusions. But I did not quarrel with the way in which people wished to interpret the tears in my eyes.

Chapter 302

Even now I find that almost all those people who talk to me about those incomparable days are usually doing their best to conceal a smirk which infallibly lets me know that they are really thinking about the moment when I tripped as I was ceremonially going up the fabulous stairway. Isn't that typical!

You campaign for your country for 45 years, and all people remember is a single moment when you fell on your face.

Chapter 303

However, when I was a child, grown women were already talking to boys in a motherly manner – and I have no reason to doubt even for a moment that they are still doing it now. For it is notorious how easy it is for a woman to keep a secret.

Chapter 304

Even so: whenever I suspect that my view of my own centrality – or of the somehow greater reality of the particular atom of time within which I bombinate – I try to counteract it by artificial means. Something is missing there, isn't it?

131

Chapter 305

That is to say, I attempt to conjure up an image of two vast armies facing each other and in rough battle formation, but with everyone, certainly up to and including the rank of Major (or equivalent), either asleep, drunk or masturbating.

If this fails, which it often does, I then uncork one of the more distant apertures of my brain, which is fermented underwater (pay close attention to this incoherence if you wish), and next, jealous of the superfluousness of past sunrises, we waken up together in the morning almost laughing. She is wearing my pyjamas and I am running across a nearby bridge, followed by a dog carrying a brassière in his mouth.

(Let us not investigate this – or indeed any other – fleeting image too closely. Let us chastely observe that by its consistent, pointless barking throughout the entire night, it has scarcely endeared itself to many people in the neighbourhood.)

Chapter 306

Next, I pause (alone) at an immediately encountered doorway – either because I am out of breath, or because I am helplessly shitting planetoids – a most embarrassing sort of thing to happen in public.

Chapter 307

Or perhaps I have stubbed my toe against social inequality, and I must wait until the initial agonising pain subsides.

Chapter 308

As I raise my eyes to the heavens, I see that they are full of oversized heads.

You know, I do not think I would have minded quite so much had not so many of them been obviously enjoying themselves.

Chapter 309

The occasional one was even drinking a viciously potent cheap liquor.

Chapter 310

Very well, I thought, and I went right into the next shop, to buy something to drink.

Chapter 311

Frankly, I was horrified by the scene of social deprivation which I saw there. It was from this moment that I date a turning-point in my life. (And who would dare to deny that our lives are the precipitate of a million indifferent minds?)

Chapter 312

No-one, I think I may safely claim, who has seen a few dozen mournful old-age pensioners being sodomized by a set of small almost lethally unintelligible leaflets, is liable ever to forget the experience. Certainly, I left the establishment shocked – vowing never again even to touch alcohol. The love of alcohol, I now sincerely believe, is basically a particularly vicious form of incest.

Chapter 313

From now on, I thought, I am a new man. I will confine myself solely to the diluted recycled urine of my wife, if I can ever find her.

Chapter 314

However, a soldier promptly followed me out and began to make monstrous suggestions – forgetting that I had the power to make meteors fall on people.

Chapter 315

Thus evening passed, and morning, and eventually the Edinburgh bus arrived after all, but nobody got off it, somewhat to my surprise.

Chapter 316

So I wiped the tears from my eyes and went back home.

Chapter 317

And where, I hear you enquire, is that home? I shall tell you. For one reason or another I have always throughout my entire life taken up domicile – or seem to have done so (motivated by what strange fate or destiny I know not) – within sight of what might laughingly be called the major educational institutions and establishments of our country.

My present abode is especially well-endowed in this respect.

Look – from this window I can observe a gateway of great historical distinction to its owners and occupiers.

Chapter 318

Thus, I observe this morning – nearly afternoon now – another long burst of graduates, wearing formal coloured cloaks and carrying cased scrolls, disembouche onto an adjunct of the public highway.

Look at them – they think the world is just beginning. (A strange attitude to adopt when leaving a 500 year-old building!) And what lights of pride in their parents' eyes!

Chapter 319

At least, I assume they are their parents. Doubtless so do they.

Chapter 320

Ah – that noise indicates that my dinner is ready.

Chapter 321

I shall eat it, and return to the window, unworried by this recombination of a once alert and proud rodent, and will discover that all these people have disappeared.

Chapter 322

However, as the day is not yet over, perhaps another group will have taken their place – equally proud, suspecting nothing of the former group which I, from my godlike lair, have seen.

Chapter 323

I eat my dinner.

Chapter 324

Oh – there is a last one! A charming straggler!

She hurries out of the gateway, looks to left and right.

What, my dear – was the excitement too much for you? A few restful, recuperative moments in the ladies' toilets were needed, were they? Have no fears: I will tell no-one. I will tell no-one of you by name, and trust that others will prove to be equally reticent.

And indeed: since you are almost entirely invented, how could they not prove to be so?

Chapter 325

I wonder if she is a doctor. I am slightly worried by these repeated slow curving pains in the back that I have begun to get. These, alas, are not invented.

Chapter 326

Perhaps the immensely subtle structure of my body – mysterious even to myself who thus systematically or accidentally abuses it – would be fairly well-known to her, to a mind somewhere about those fluttering and no doubt sensationally scented curls – particularly if it should correspond at all accurately to a few thousand I suppose necessarily idealized diagrams.

Chapter 327

Ah! Another twinge of pain!

Or does she know instead – perhaps even in addition! – all about, say, the soft drift of frozen smoke over the once so nearly so very nearly vibrant canyons of Mars?

Or the endless sea which once covered all these points – that road, that wall, that line of windows – where for so long none too aware jaws snapped, and where certificates were not remotely thought necessary?

But I suppose she is probably just a lawyer, like almost all of these transients.

Chapter 328

Suddenly, she starts into life. She hurries across the road, my angelic little beauty, and disappears out of sight directly below my house.

Oh, I know what you are after, madam, but you won't get it, oh no – certainly not from me! I am not so easily caught – though I would not therefore counsel you to give in to the sin of despair, as so many theologians prefer to call rational thought.

Chapter 329

Listen! I expect she is climbing the stairway outside at this very minute. Softly now. Softly. Can you hear her?

Soon she will be breaking into my apartment, and will beg me (with adorable tears in her tender young eyes) to rip open her gown (lined with coloured silks whose significance is a mystery to me) and implore me, with her tears rather suspiciously by now beginning to dry up, to beat her frenziedly about the hinder parts with that large scroll newly handed to her in recognition of her mental achievements or powers of memory, at present still fondled with so much pride, even though in a decade or two it might well be lost or hidden away in a cupboard somewhere beneath some unregarded wedding photographs.

Isn't it always exactly the same?

Chapter 330

Actually, it would be more accurate to ask, isn't it always exactly different? But, whatever it is, you have got the wrong person entirely, madam! Yes, indeed. Little can you guess what fortitude of mind I at least possess. No! I refuse. No! I am adamant! Utterly adamant! Particularly after those so recent shattering events! Ah, let me see! Can I still remember them? How sadly unpredictable they all are! No!

I refuse. There is absolutely no use in begging. There is no use imploring. Believe me, I will simply continue to ignore that knocking at the door. Can I still remember those terrible events?

Chapter 331

Yes; it seems I can. It started as one of those apparently nondescript afternoons which seem to delight in masquerading as any of a billion identical instances before and after. I am sure you know the sort I mean.

I had long since decided to expect nothing particular from it. Nonetheless, it is possible that in reality I continued to expect something. I must puzzle over this a little longer. Must I? Who cares?

Chapter 332

A car pulled by me, preparing to halt at nearby traffic-lights. It was driven by a remarkably attractive young blonde or pseudoblonde woman – and I could see from her face that she was talking volubly.

But who was she talking to?

Chapter 333

That unspoken question was answered almost at once; for, leaning over the back of her seat from the rear of the car was another female much like her, albeit in a younger, scaled-down version.

So they went on talking in the slowing-down car.

Chapter 334

At the lights, where they had stopped, I walked past them, achieving as I did so a clear view of the two similar, active heads, which were talking away at each other.

Chapter 335

The woman exchanged a look with me as I passed. It was only as she gave this look that I realized I still knew who she was.

Chapter 336

My mind, or something else, leapt back to a superb spring morning 23 years before – when her mother and I had been out in the garden of her fine house in one of the pleasanter suburbs. You probably know its name, and equally probably its sort.

We had been up all night, and we had seen in the earliest hours of the morning by various delightful ruses and reminiscences.

There had also been a certain amount of gambling going on, of a moderate and at times predominantly psychological nature.

Chapter 337

And a certain amount of gambolling too, I suppose.

Chapter 338

Thus it was that I was standing by the back-door of the house, breathing in the invigorating still slightly cool air, and occasionally (only occasionally) shying away from newly-arriving insects whose motives were none too clear to me.

Of the dazzling flowers I have surprisingly little to say.

I had however, I clearly remember, grown tired of committing loving indignities upon her delightful body, which I fear I did not soon enough learn to treasure as much as I should have done.

Chapter 339

Nonetheless, I found one moment duly arriving when my attention was attracted or distracted by what I can only call (since I have forgotten all the other words) a modest repetitive percussive sound nearby. This caused me to look over to where her own small daughter, who could not yet drive a car, was standing, and I discovered that she was, by the use of an extremely substantial but flexible slat, eight centimetres wide and eighteen metres long – clearly the neck vertebrae of some or other extinct form of life – furiously and with I would have thought impossible zeal belabouring precisely something which I would love to be able to recall, but alas, at this point, most unfortunately, my stoic and insufficiently resilient memory utterly fails me. What shards and relics, I hear you ask, remain? Let me try to rescue what I can.

Chapter 340

I seem to remember her as kneeling, which is perhaps impossible – rather than as sprawled forwards ungainlyly onto her face. No no – there was nothing ungainly about any of it; of that I am sure. Nor was there anything undignified, or destructive, or cruel, or inconsistent and out of keeping with the exquisite stately dignity of such a human being as she (or both) once was. That much remains clear to me.

It was, spiritually, a most satisfying and thought-provoking moment for all concerned.

Chapter 341

I have, of course, changed one or two hundred of the details to make it less recognisable to those (of whom I am fairly certain there are depressingly few) who can understand exactly what it is that I am talking about – though not, I hope, less plausible than the reality actually was. And I have left out the leaping and talking hosepipe entirely. Likewise the little black bow. Nevertheless, the situation in essence took place as I have described it, except that it is well over 90% imaginary. Truly, where would any of us be without all these vignettes of ordinary family life?

Chapter 342

As I say, my eyes and the daughter's met 27 years later, and I sensed in them instantly a genuine nostalgia for the events of so long ago.

Chapter 343

It would be pure guesswork on my part to attempt to surmise what she in her turn might have read into my eyes. But when the lights changed in her favour, as they did almost at once, the car sped away with an outrageous acceleration that I strongly suspected was not completely normal. Nonetheless, on the following afternoon I found myself round at her bafflingly unfamiliar house, and we proceeded to have a most interesting discussion. I must admit that I found it, and especially what followed it, to be extremely surprising.

Chapter 344

It is all the more surprising when we remember that the first family was a flat stone on which balanced a trembling throat, not far away from a small dullish star and a large single bed. Mercilessly, the sun beats down upon the stone for several multiples of 73 million years – an activity which it interrupts only once – to throw gently a small pair of decorated underpants onto them, thereby sheltering them a little from the scorching heat. We must take our respite, unlike our joy, wherever we can find it. After all, where else will we find it – particularly if we in any way belong to that group known as 'poets', who are nothing if not the frilly panties of History.

Chapter 345

Of course, there is not yet any sound of talking, or of dogs barking. Have I already mentioned that there is already a pair of cups there? I should have done so, for the wind has just knocked it over. And it is on actions such as this, on actions no more significant than this, that new religions are or were founded. And with the birth of religion comes the birth of surrealism.

Chapter 346

For what other sort of actions are there? Let us be explicit for once: none. Or do you disagree? Why should you not disagree? It is, after all, whether I or you am alive or not, a strange world. Yet how could there exist an unstrange world? Consider, for instance, the motley assortment of people who disturb my brain every morning, improbable as the chance groupings in public transport vehicles – which is usually what they try to present themselves, unconvincingly, as being. Nonetheless, we all know that underground trains are merely a more restrained form of brothel.

Chapter 347

But I am travelling on it nonetheless, in the company of many people who wakened up – out of sleep or whatever it was – less than an hour ago.

Our faces are like doors swinging open and shut with no-one entering and no-one leaving. Our hands struggle not to touch our neighbours or our faces or our neighbours' faces. Our pain is as subtle as the scent of the recent dawn (for what does it matter what colour the clouds are, so long as the rain is falling?), or as stratospherically threatening as the pillars which hold up the roof of the sky, or, less problematically, this coach.

Each time we look up, different people are gazing at us, appalled.

Chapter 348

I got out at the station at which I had intended to get out, which is slightly unusual for me, for I am a known (or obvious) eccentric. I at once raced back along a superb row of bright sunlit houses, all of which (pointing out the directions help-fully) led me to the previous station.

Chapter 349

Here I got onto the next train. (I am fortunate in having the precise ticket which allows me to do this). I then repeated the aforementioned process exactly. Ah! It was like suddenly discovering that one's parents really were heterosexual after all. A rare discovery indeed!

Chapter 350

I repeated this procedure throughout the entire morning. Eventually it brought forth the result which I was seeking.

Chapter 351

Arriving on the next train for the 8th time, astonished as ever to find new people there, inhabitants of my own city, yet not a single one of whom I recognised – I recognised a woman who was sheltering, perhaps even cowering, in the shallow alcove beside the doorway at the opposite extremity of the coach to where I was standing. She has been trying to ignore me for the last 12 years, and now blind chance has thrown us together!

Chapter 352

As has increasingly become my habit recently, I farted from delight – and at that moment (sheer coincidence, I assume) the electrical lighting system within the train failed, which plunged us all into amplified breathing and slurping noises in the surrounding darkness.

During this brief period of profundity, I perhaps went mad to a certain extent.

Chapter 353

But, all the same, I was not so mad that I failed to notice, when the lights came on again, that the woman by the alcove had disappeared and had been replaced by a cauliflowerperson – which is to say, by an otherwise quite ordinary female, whose lovely head had become a peculiarly luscious example of that, in other circumstances, none too interesting vegetable.

Chapter 354

As I whispered to her, the occasional crisp leaf fell from her head softly to the ground – a sure sign of arousal on her part.

Chapter 355

Thus it was that, less than 45 seconds later, we made our way up the distinctive arching stairway of St Criscross's Station. She was still (as if unwilling to admit the truth even to herself) weakly seeking to invent excuses for our not following this particular course of action.

Chapter 356

To my surprise (but not, it seems, to hers) it was raining steadily.

Chapter 357

Therefore we went to a room which I kept nearby; rented but friendly; rarely visited, but not cold; actual, but not windswept; ugly but not grief-filled; containing flimsy shoes, but not eternal. In short, the locus of certain of the happiest moments of my life – although often empty for long consecutives of days and weeks and nights and minutes. (One of the chief problems is, I keep forgetting where it is.)

Chapter 358

Of course, the resilient body tissue of females is often too beautiful to seem veridical. Particularly so if cars are passing in long loud swishing lines outside the window. Whereas, if something which is not merely a plasticated facsimile of such objects is moving, not to say swaying, to a certain extent in an atmosphere of subdued music, horrorstruck vengeful gratitude, light slowed to a near standstill, and the infinite subtleties of an area near a single shoulder, then realism and good taste alike demand that one simply be silent at once.

Chapter 359

So I tried. And yet, merely by looking at the room one would never think that an astonishing battle had once taken place in it. Or don't you agree?

Chapter 360

Looking at another human being is much the same. Or don't you agree?

Chapter 361

Or, to put it another way – a single mistake and anyone's life is different, or non-existent, or ruined. Which is presumably why you are not here.

Chapter 362

A single mistake and the brain refuses to form. Nobody nurses you. Therefore nobody misses you.

Chapter 363

Rather, though not exactly as, a single moment's inadvertence at a machine – a machine like this for instance – and everything that one has written for weeks (which are parts of centuries) disappears and cannot be retraced. But do you not know that I miss you? Was my recent behaviour not sufficient to let you know that?

Chapter 364

And yet, it has already happened to the earth several times, and will do so again. *That* we can hardly doubt. Who misses the original stars? No-one. But now other things genuinely miss other things.

Chapter 365

But the moment everything disappears – what a sense of freedom!

Chapter 366

Or rather – since there is no sense existing, let us simply say – what freedom! But there are some freedoms which they are at liberty to keep.

Chapter 367

For who would not prefer to be tied into time with you? If it is a sort of tying.

Chapter 368

Or could it be the case that beauty itself is perhaps a cage which she or someone like her is trapped within? That is something which I wondered about fleetingly as I woke up in yet another morning and found that she had not quite disappeared. A moderate light shone upon me, and I heard a distant but compelling voice speaking to me from within it. It asked me if I knew what time it was, then it added something about eggs. Although confused, I replied with the eminently sane observation that (in the end) everything was about eggs.

Chapter 369

Later in the week, I asked my father what was the German for a wheelbarrow.

Chapter 370

But no – that had been in the previous year, when he was still alive. Women were hurrying through the garden, and, at their passing, the tall stone statues of nude heroes cracked into pieces, and crashed to the ground in one colossal piece of debris after another.

Chapter 371

Not that it matters much. In the evening we could hear the lassies outside giggling as they gathered various disjecta membra and put them into a large cardboard box. They stole away silently, before 8 o'clock in the evening. I watched as the setting sun sniffed the valley of the nearby semi-industrial streamlet, as a weary God might sniff a Goddess's oxter, before suggesting to her, with a diffidence appropriate to such a superb otherwordly occasion, that she really ought not to shave away such in her case elegant tracery work, as beauty in the world (and after all, the more myopic a man is, the more he rails against women's beauty) was too precarious to be dispelled in however modest a degree.

Chapter 372

All that, of course, was merely a description of a particularly pleasant tune coming from the radio. I switched it off, and not only because it was too beautiful. For let us be frank: what astonishing things may not happen when a man and a woman can only be left alone in a Paradise with nothing for company but a couple of bananas.

Chapter 373

Or perhaps you would prefer a dishonest confession. Very well, in that case listen to this – personally I abhor abominate and detest music. Do you wish to know why? Because it closes too many windows, not to mention too many lives. It also makes me too aware of the likelihood that our concept of the dead has never been able to twitch its legs as it obviously should.

Chapter 374

This tends to so depress me that even the laughter of the peculiarly likeable children next door cannot prevent me from falling into the usual melancholy stupor which is almost as musical and as unnecessary as a miniature waterfall in Wester Ross long before the latest Ice Age, which I used to know a lot about, but have sadly forgotten.

Chapter 375

Very well. I swim through its chill waters, nude apart from my elaborate, helpfully light earrings. This goes on for a very long time, but my strength never deserts me, though I nearly drown perhaps slightly more often I would ideally choose to do.

Chapter 376

At length, towards evening, I drag myself out of the water at what is a pleasantly sheltered, but in no way exceptional part of the shore.

I see a light in the distance, as usual.

Chapter 377

However, as is my normal reaction whenever I am in the grip of a less than reliable erection, I had considerable difficulty in seeing where it is that I was going to.

Chapter 378

This surprised me all the more in that, until then, I had typically thought of myself as being a woman.

Chapter 379

Anyway, a walk of an hour or so brings me to pleasantly beaded windows. I gaze through them, alert and sure of myself.

Chapter 380

At first it is difficult to distinguish anything of what is happening inside – but then, as the eyes get used to the perfectly natural brightness, they begin to make out what looks uncannily like a long line of unexceptional rodents, distinguishable from the normal only in that many are apparently brainless, and that, after unpredictable intervals of a few seconds or millenia or whatever the momentarily preferred term is, the brain of yet another one would likewise disappear.

Chapter 381

I must admit that it seemed to me at once that it would be unwise to blame this sort of phenomenon wholly on the weather. With noble heart, I thrust open the door, and went in as if I were in a world where pusillanimity was impossible (however much one liked the word) – although to this day I much regret that as I did so I all too obviously wilted with fear.

A little old comb sitting in an occluded corner of the room was watching me with some interest. I think you may have something I need, she said to me flirtatiously – insofar as one can be genuinely flirtatious with blood dripping from one's teeth.

Chapter 382

She held a mirror to my face, and I was astonished and, yes, horrified by what I saw.

Chapter 383

And even more so, of course, by what I failed to see. For it has become more and more often the case now that I chance to glimpse one of my great-great-grandfathers staring back at me out of those mirrors which I fail to prevent myself from noticing in time.

Chapter 384

And I realize with sadness that ordinary events will remain to me as baffling as extraordinary ones, until that point in a drizzling wet afternoon when I wholly disappear while a few people perhaps weep momentarily, among vast clouds or I should rather say vast crowds who are shitting, saying "What?", "Where?", and "Who?", or shopping for fleeting, exaggerated bargains.

Chapter 385

Somebody is talking in the street outside. A tree waves slightly above a wall. A child runs by the almost stationary wall. 50 years later, an adult is running (or is trying to run) past the wall.

We might call it the same wall.

Chapter 386

We might call it the same person. Nonetheless, afternoon sunlight is cutting lines on the ground, whether or not the person I love is alive or dead or, through something extremely simple just not happening, never existed. (I, of course, suspect the last to have been untrue.) So someone peeps round a distant corner, looking to see if anyone else is there.

Chapter 387

Someone else is usually there. In more sunlit afternoons than there have been women. One infinity would have been enough to defeat me. What joy is there is defeating us with more? And, if joy, then for whom? After all, those who call Evolution 'God' are only talking about Evolution.

And now those rainy afternoons, like this one, which seem set to go on absolutely for ever, and perhaps somewhere do (No!), but not here, not here.

Chapter 388

Look at that! Exactly the same scene confronts me as the one I saw yesterday. How much I now regret being immured behind this particularly thick type of wall, unable almost to speak for love, unable to do anything but live. But live and hear and see, I mean.

Chapter 389

A mother is teaching her child to talk. Oh, rare optimism!

Chapter 390

What – can that child be mine too? The puzzlingly knowing way in which it looks towards me suggests an answer to this interrogative which is definitely inclined towards the positive. Ah, the sunlight! There is sunlight too!

Chapter 391

I am undoubtedly reluctant to stretch the knicker-elastic of narrative or the universe further than it can reasonably be made to go (let me confess that I sometimes fear that I may have done so already), but honesty compels me to point out that neither of the females whom I am watching is asleep, for they are talking to each other, answering questions, and looking out of the window towards the to me disconcertingly unnecessary people who are passing by on the road outside.

Chapter 392

Time, then, to step forward bravely out of this prison! What? Can I still not move? This leg perhaps? No. This leg? No. This knee which seemed so recently to acquire from I know not where an unsightly, possibly malign growth? I begin to heave. Other parts of my body twitch and creak. I am disintegrating; I am disintegrating – but with a striking absence of panic. What a catharsis! Am I to go without ever having properly arrived?

Chapter 393

Before I quite disappear, however, after the fashion of so many entities which have hitherto esteemed themselves, deluded by normality and the continuing power of the automatic reflex, to be inviolably eternal sovereign states, let me first, indomitable as the superb endeavours of a true-hearted philosopher who has struggled for decades to have his wife's buttocks (I originally wrote "nose", but I am reluctant to appear obsessed) to be declared a sovereign state, with its right to its own army, flag, coinage, and international representation, including the sensible, progressive deployment of at least ten or so accredited, competent diplomats, let me recall the final terse discussion that we had then.

Chapter 394

She began by pointing out that even if we lived for several billions of years each, we should all die eventually (and only once) nonetheless. I did not demur. How could I have done so with truth? But I did remark that it would surely be a consolation of sorts to see the mountains changing – instead of merely reading (as is now the usual somewhat demeaning practice) that such things are the case, far too slow for our limited eyes, etc., to see. Her own response was tripartite. That mountains cannot live. That their structure is too rigid. How could blood flow through them?

Chapter 395

We would see the constellations drifting apart too. I am not quite sure whether or not I would like to see that. But it would be visible. Presumably it already is.

Chapter 396

If we looked away from the sky, she said, then looked back 74 or 75 million years later, for no particular reason. Rather like observing a nephew unexpectedly growing up.

Chapter 397

The fact that we expected it would not make it so very much less unexpected, I think. Otherwise it would merely be a slow drift, like our faces, which are usually more charming than the ability of a certain bird to issue its sharp piercing monotonous one-note call of (I presume) warning from 4.15 until 5.25 a.m. without the least intermission, woundingly uninterested in the proximity of an ill-sleeping local nexus of devastating verbal ability.

Chapter 398

We would soon, it was pointed out, refuse utterly to look at the stars, as did the founder of psychoanalysis, who was at one time thought to be a sage, but who never quite managed to realize that no woman is half-a-dozen golden rings sparkling in a dish. We would drift on the continents. We would see different mesmerizing varieties of birds descend from the skies.

Chapter 399

I like the word "skies", I said. But what are they different from? (Different from those who took to the air, of course, silly. And life would seem too short. Even though half an hour can easily seem too long – as it did only yesterday on three quite distinct occasions.)

Chapter 400

Presumably we would be changing too, she asked, making me see all too keenly how dangerous it is to compare women to windows.

Chapter 401

Of course, I replied. We change anyway, my darling. We were once smaller than that tiny dot there on your neck. Or even that other one just beside it. Why you worry about such things in the least mystifies me. And we were once inside a tiny sac itself inside a woman's body which itself got in and out of elevators – were we not – even though we fly in jets tomorrow over the roofs. Jets and pterodactyls both decay.

Chapter 402

But passengers do not disembark from pterodactyls, I replied.

Chapter 403

That depends more than anything on your point of view, someone said. Perhaps pterodactyls disembarked from pterodactyls. After all, I mean to say: if we lived for only a split-second – and who is to claim with overwhelming confidence that in fact we don't – then rainfall would be a sky full of apparently motionless planets.

Chapter 404

I seemed to remember hearing that being said before, but I simply couldn't remember where and when. But we do live for only a split-second, do we not, I asked. Isn't that why so many find the experience meaningless?

Chapter 405

Is that why they do it? I thought it might be because we live for ever.

Chapter 406

Was that why? I can never remember which is which.

Chapter 407

Oh, look! Something is happening over there, as usual. And so we did look – for we have always had a sneaking sympathy for lizards – who, after all, have tried so hard for millenia to become as subtle and likeable as women's tongues, and have failed so spectacularly in their noble attempt.

Chapter 408

Thus it was that I chanced to remember what had occurred the last time I had jumped over such a wall, trying to escape my inescapable pursuer. But first you must bear in mind certain facts. I had been hiding behind a plant for 4 minutes or so, and the gruesome distant commotion had almost died away entirely, when the door of the next house regally opened and various people in superb finery began to descend the main stairway onto the broad stone path below, near which I stood, trembling. It seemed to me that the entire family had gathered together for some reason or other.

Chapter 409

I did not recognise any of them. A couple of the older ones halted near where I was tremulously ensconced, and I was privileged to overhear their sotto voce remarks, which either discussed distant stellar forms or were of a rare frankness.

Chapter 410

Judge of my horror, however, when I at length realized, in an unease which gradually precipitated into a flash of inspiration, that the bushes behind which I had imagined myself to be hiding were in fact at the other end of the garden entirely; and that, thus, anyone who happened to look towards me must see me. If I had really been born by then, the consequences must necessarily have been horrendous.

True, a dog began to bark just at that instant; but no-one paid it the slightest attention, fortunately for me.

Chapter 411

Of course, I was not the dog in any shape. Nor was that animal me. How could it be? After all, nothing is or was me. Or am I perchance wrong here again? Might it not perhaps indeed be true, as I think Knox so memorably put it, that they also serve the general purpose who only sit about in a relative's bedroom with the curtains drawn, fighting the temptation to masturbate?

Chapter 412

It may be so. How else can I understand why I should have thought that I have been here before – as I did while I walked through the opened doorway for the first time at such a peculiar point in the day.

Chapter 413

As I returned home, I had passed in the street near my house (far nearer to me than you are now) the woman who surely ought to have been my wife. What annals we would have made possible! Why did I not talk to her? Stupidity, I suppose.

Chapter 414

Or, if I did, why did I not say something more interesting?

Chapter 415

Yet the rooms are all as I remember them. But let me merely console myself with the thought that almost none of us were produced as the result of an overwhelming passion.

Chapter 416

And, in truth, I no longer pine uselessly for those glorious years when the lives and hopes and weeks around me were much straighter.

When they did not, as it were, bend in towards me and others with the pressure that they use now.

Nor am I as eager to find lost or perfect children as perhaps you are. For now life has wrinkled up beside the fire of a star and has fallen into a dreamless sleep. I am only one of the eyes of fleas which looks slyly out from between strands of its fabric. Thus it is that I slip on my jacket and glide out into the noisy, laborious, shriek-filled night, trying to be as silent as possible.

This is not as easy as I, or one, might wish.

Chapter 417

For of late it seems that there is always something appalling happening over in that direction, where the distance-markers march down the sky like a troop of humanely-shackled prisoners.

Occasional feathers flutter onto the paving-stones, and not only where there are paving-stones. The unseen types of wolf race along the minor highway, barking or discussing religion sporadically, on their way to some fairly uninteresting destination known only to them.

A door opens into the world, and they run through it.

Chapter 418

Let us leap onwards a little. Trees appear, one after the other, as if there were a reason for each of them.

Chapter 419

It is much the same for extremely old women, even those who have finally shaken free of the troubling beauties of an elderly nun soaking langorously in a bath. Take that one, for instance.

Chapter 420

She is hiding under a stellar cloud thrown briefly over her head, in the shadow of a tree which has not yet been cut down and made into a single one of those utterly innumerable handbooks which nowadays come with so many things – whether it be cars, or weapons, or lawnmowers, or sexual aids, or word processors. (I deliberately limit myself to naming only three categories here.) Perhaps we too feel that, ideally, we ought to come with handbooks of our own. We feel there ought to be one for us lying about somewhere, but we are never able to find the damn thing. Our suspicion however is that other people have all read theirs. A male also tends to have the additional suspicion that women have already skimmed through his own, and have not been frightfully impressed. But enough of these eternal digressions, enchanting as a delightful infant whom I would greatly regret accidentally killing by attaching a time-bomb to his larynx, primed to detonate on the 1,115th occasion when he gives a thrilling scream somewhere (but alas not far enough, never far enough) in the distance on what otherwise might have been such a beautiful morning.

Chapter 421

So, let us at once dismiss the unimportant question: why is she there – particularly if she used to refuse to show enough of her gleeful bust to a slightly important and greatly desperate man over 130 million years ago. Is it enough to know that there has been a dreadful accident in every quiet lane of the locality?

Chapter 422

You understand, I take it, that I do not suggest that you are in the lane (or indeed anywhere else) at the present moment? Perhaps you yourself once hurried down such a lane, not unlike my father, perhaps pursued by a legitimately disgusted mob? But if this is not you, then no doubt it is someone else – although, actually, I strongly suspect that it is you. After all, you are a known liar and a hypocrite, aren't you?

Chapter 423

Perhaps I went too far. If I did so, do forgive me. I thought it really might as well have been you, but I could be wrong. I could be wrong about that too. I am certainly tired.

Perhaps it was me. But I am tired of being everyone. I'm sorry: that is almost the opposite of what I meant to say. It always is. Let me merely state the irrefutable fact that there is no general duty incumbent upon all human beings, except perhaps that of ruthlessly killing insects whenever the opportunity arises, and let me go into this neighbouring room instead.

Chapter 424

How may I best describe it? A roomful of happy people. An empty room.

And those are my youngest days. Or an empty room.

And this here must be a space for joy, which would have accepted mere happiness easily enough. Who is that, if anyone, hiding in the corner?

Something runs out into the sunlight. But the sunlight is not there for long either. And in the end, all one can object to is the universe. Let us console ourselves with the thought that if Life were possible, it would probably be unbearable.

Chapter 425

Of course the original oceans are not still here either. What does it matter that you cannot imagine where else they can have got to? It is not a question of what you imagine. Only the strength of my scarcely sufficiently commendable distaste for tyranny enables me to withstand the force of the suggestion that people should be compelled to carry a picture of the circumstances of their own birth with them wherever they go – for the good of their sense of proportion in particular, and their ludicrous aspirations after certainty in general.

I do not concede that this is necessarily of little help in regard to dealing with those beautiful faces that neither you nor anyone else will ever again see. Perhaps it is true that no-one recognises love. But no-one can be ruined by women who would not have been worse ruined by the absence of women!

Chapter 426

Yet, from any window I can see that people continue to walk down this road or that road with a nonchalance that seems grossly out of keeping with the radial velocity of the earth, a fairly small planet. Or of the sun too, for that matter – an extremely small star. But we can get used to anything – even overwhelmingly deep or merely big eyes. How true it is that women are what stars would be if stars were women! That love is the anus of God's sister-in-law I would take to be a more troublesome proposition however.

Chapter 427

At times the immense distances seem further away than ever. I simply cannot believe that I have looked out of other people's windows as often as I have actually done. Is it as often as I should have done? Can such things ever be so?

Chapter 428

Even out of my own one I was often enough surprised – seeing things move which I had thought were stable. Or doing nearly nothing, which I had nonetheless allowed myself to believe might be the sort of person capable of understanding me.

Chapter 429

Perhaps my greatest sorrow is that it took me so long to find an absent-minded universe truly convincing. Am I to be blamed for this? What is ultimate knowledge but a final opinion which happens to be held immediately prior to extinction? Could I not simply blame you instead? And my greatest joy?

Chapter 430

What joy? Now I am less than those two people – if it is only two people – whispering in a bed in a corner of a shadowy music-filled room which still retains some of the distinctive scent of a cheap food. Memories are in this room here and now. In what other sort of place could they be?

Chapter 431

Why worry? Perhaps 45% of experience is put to good use. The light breeze dies away anyway.

(Not the one from the sun. The other one. Someone is breathing beside me.)

Chapter 432

History is a surface so complicated that it looks like infinite depth. In this it is hardly misleading. What (I asked her) if some researcher of genius were to take a single cell from my body and a single cell from yours, and were to cause them to be combined? Who would that other person be? (After all, Man's love is weaker than Woman's, and vice-versa.)

She replied, but I forget what she said. It was something frightening about another person. The world shook again, as it had done at the very start.

Chapter 433

And what of a cell taken from J.S Bach, linked to a cell from Shakespeare – what do you think that would produce? (So I asked, remembering that women frequently forget an injury.)

Chapter 434

That would probably produce a highly intelligent builder's labourer with a never discovered gift for dancing. As she spoke, her neck in some way quivered, suggesting that it was fully aware of the fact that all systems for understanding the world are actually attempts to create a limited world which can be understood. I should have remembered that what a woman thinks is what a woman thinks.

Chapter 435

Since the planet had indeed once begun – unless it has always been there, where (which?) I doubt – we continued our sexual discussion. There was also the erotic noise of a car passing nearby, which can sound extremely like a car, especially if someone is laughing in the room at the same time.

(I have noticed that laughter in other rooms does not have quite the same effect).

Chapter 436

But the shuffle of genes which produced you (I shrieked at the height of my passion) could conceivably just as easily have produced any single one of a billion billion billion other people – many of whom I would probably have been very glad to be here with. If anything, I am underestimating things in this connection.

Chapter 437

And yet, how charming I find your smile. Where else would it be, if not here? And those eyes! Oh, what a knack human beings have of changing into other things! Have I already said that I fear that neither men nor women deserve each other? Then let me merely point out that males and females probably exist so that each sex has another one to blame.

Chapter 438

Nonetheless, war between the sexes is civil war. And even the nearly infinite universe has not enough space for those other people who could be sitting in your chair there.

And not on those glorious knees either, for they would be entirely lost. Or rather, they would never have been found. So what then is this battering not for the first time at what I can only describe as my loving heart?

Chapter 439

What am I to say to all those other people who could be here sipping my glass of milk? Oh, God! (Forgive me this ejaculation. I am well aware that few sounds are as deafening as the silence in which one hallucinates the non-existent voice of a non-existent incoherent entity such as most sophisticated – that is to say, not obviously refuted – versions of God might be. For what does prayer most commonly consist of, but in begging the non-existent to do that which he could not do even if he were to exist? But I suspect that Man's love for God is a natural result of that rather pleasing human sympathy for the has-been. Or would be so, if indeed he had ever been there in the first place. Yet it is a little strange that we should feel the necessity for inventing imaginary Gods, when real vaginas exist.)

Chapter 440

Unfortunately, I have forgotten in the course of my latest digression exactly what I was going to ask the Almighty. Since the concept is a superfluous one, that is not entirely inappropriate. But let me not try to brazen things out by speculating on what else the milk could be. After all, it could not be our happiness. It could not even be our sudden noticing of the sunlight after the heavy, somewhat depressing rainfall of the two previous days. Let us not investigate this further.

Chapter 441

After all, if we had not met, we would (obviously) not be talking to each other. And if we had not existed, then only other people would have been talking.

And if we had not evolved, much that same sunlight would still have more or less been shining.

And if the sun had collapsed, I would still be sitting here in this room, admiring a part of your body which you genuinely seem to wish had been somewhat different – a bizarre train of thought to evolve in anyone, it seems to me.

Chapter 442

At least one of these statements is not true, I admit. And if things had been otherwise, where would anyone be able to find your endearing but quite unnecessary wish that things could have been otherwise?

Chapter 443

Perhaps I ought not to have asked that. It may well be the case that, in a sense, we are all stranded on planets occupied by inadequacies. Sometimes they change into scaled animals, and slouch off irrespective of their predecessors' wishes. Of course, we (their owners) have often enough slipped away to hilly, picturesque, tree-lined villages, where we have glimpsed centuries resting in the branches of trees, pausing before embarking on a longer journey. They are holding some of our rainy schooldays in their talons, or merely in their claws.

Chapter 444

Does it sometimes seem as if a God is inflating our morning unmercifully? Let us hope the birds can fly out of them without bursting its fabric with their sharp claws. Yes, off they go, lifting up wearily into the sky. But the claws dig in, and trickles of blood begin to run down our faces. Our past cannot thus run down our faces, although perhaps it is inside us too. What strange birds continue to fly through it.

Chapter 445

A few more traces of blood in a garden. Does anybody even notice them by now? Is that me? Is that you? All those barely glimpsed faces. A few marks. No-one knows of their potentialities or possibilities. An entire population is lost in each blade of grass, through no more than a moment's inattention. But what is it thus gnaws at the back of my mind? Something heard before? Said before? Done before?

Chapter 446

Yes. Surely I have done this before – thought the dying man, before remembering that he thought he was me. A word of advice.

Do not mistake the human voice for a birdcall. Nor for a deep subterranean avalanche. Nor for an orbit, whether irregular or not. Nor for that point in the distance where parallel lines meet.

Also, avoid the exactly intermediate points.

The present is the present in a different shape. Actually, I meant to say that the present is the past in a different shape, but I am loth to lose my mistakes.

After all: if we lost our mistakes, how much would we be left with?

Chapter 447

No matter how fast we speed, we will never reach it. And no matter how slowly we walk either. Nor will attempts at motionlessness, which (most treacherous of all) seem to succeed, do us much good in the end, which is to say, now. For which of us has never, perhaps in the dread silent hours of night, given in to the temptation to glance furtively to left and right, and then ostentatiously take out his penis and wave it furiously up and down in front of Almighty God or the nearest real thing to such a phantasm?

(Of course, I include females in this description.)

Chapter 448

How could I do otherwise, given that ultimately music is quite possibly the delight in female cleavage transposed into air-waves? So asked the half-drunk thinker as he watched his colleague try to balance a minor planet on his nose and, inevitably, fail.

Both got up shortly afterwards and left, sniggering at a private joke – or life, as it is sometimes called.

I myself was sorely tempted to go out just after them.

All that had held me in the busy, noisy pub, sitting opposite a terminally uninteresting woman who insisted on talking on at great length about various aspects of education and its ills, was an awareness of how impolite it would have been to her pretty brain which I, on the previous evening, in an uncharacteristic moment of weakness and self-indulgence, had lovingly attempted to thrust my more or less entranced penis into and out of in a not totally inaccurate manner for half an hour or so, generating an encouraging amount of response and well-feigned delight while I attempted, as nobly as I could, to divide my attentions more or less equally between the lobes. After all, I am not the sort who minds a moderate mess – and nor was she. Quite the contrary. One must attempt to be fair. She turned out to be far less disappointed than I had first feared was likely.

Chapter 449

But to the following day! Every minute or so, with what I thought was wonderfully well-disguised ardour on my part, I would steal a furtive glance up at the quite adorable little curvaceous family of ridges and valleys, apparently charmingly unconnected to the nonsense-talking woman whose mouth so needlessly caused the air to resound far far below them. This happened so often that, in the end (just before my second glance) even *she* noticed what was going on.

Her expression took on something of the unpleasant eagerness of an ornithologist who believes himself, from certain subtle signs and stirrings in the undergrowth, to be staggeringly close to a rare, treasured species of pervert whom he has always dreamed of observing in the wild, but which he has never yet unequivocally caught sight of.

Chapter 450

Instantly, a whorl was pushed or pushed itself towards me across the table.

I ignored it as best I could.

Chapter 451

It tapped lightly against my forehead once or twice. I tried to ignore it.

It then managed to find its way, with what seemed a touching lack of expertise, down into my right hand. So I grasped her elegant little temporal lobe, and listened to her talking more or less absolute nonsense in a slightly more excited and interesting voice. Other people's conversations filled the air just beyond like thick spiral staircases. The afternoon became a child whose parents were watching it tumble and right itself, with such loving expressions that it wanted to go on doing so forever, never realizing that the faces of parents must always change.

Chapter 452

Evening was like an electric light coming on in a room in which a mirror was still reflecting something dropped an hour ago by an interesting young woman. The next day was a petal dropping off a superb flower, unseen, in a garden – and making such a noise as to disturb a small pied dog which was just about to defecate there guiltily in strict opposition to its mistress's known wishes. It scampered off, terrified.

Chapter 453

What happened later in the evening? Let me guess. A man walking on tiptoe passes in the opposite direction. What unbearable selfishness! Can he not, even for a second, try to think of anyone else? Twilight falls, if twilight can fall, and voices are almost inaudible in the nearby houses. Other planets even are very close to us for a moment, but, sensing that they are not really needed given that we know how to use our immensely complicated eyelids, they self-effacingly drift away. Well: was I right?

Chapter 454

That, however, was not the only thing that was happening. What else was happening? I (whoever I will be) shall tell you (whoever you are). Far off, in the distance (which is not necessarily the same thing, I assure you – for if women lacked ears men would hear nothing) someone is moving unseen towards you through various rooms.

Chapter 455

There is, for instance, that memorable embrace in the cut-back entrance of a modestly resonant kitchen, while a little more sunlight flickers through the dust-strewn air as equably as it flickers through the pillars of the universe, which we sense is a not hopelessly inept translation from a language which we are just about to remember. Is it not possible that the other person cannot forget it – would not, indeed, be allowed to? Why do we worry if the whole era, like a screen no longer needed, will be folded up and put away? A use has been found for it nonetheless.

Chapter 456

The door then opens with a loud noise. After I have simply said that you pass through, what next? What emerges, if not the sense of a progress through time, or perhaps a large white wave? In the sunlit doorway two silent brooding figures are thinking of the same aperture. Let us change the subject.

Chapter 457

One person here breathes out a strange gas through his nose, sadly shaking his head over the fact that we can express ourselves accurately only 3% of the time. The other (in fact there are two others) winces as a particularly sharp thrust of pain continues to assault – or, perhaps better, returns to assault – his or her urinogenitary system.

Chapter 458

Someone falls off the chair, onto the floor, gasping. After all, the sadness of others at least reassures us that the universe is not a personal conspiracy against oneself. Not that it proves anything, of course. But it makes the suggestion – that is the important thing. So a line of small-breasted women pass through the city, and as the last of them disappears through a small shared hole into history, she shuts the door in such a way that it is not clear whether she is trying to be seductive or not. But the effect is unmistakable nonetheless.

Chapter 459

Let us go on a little. Seventeen minutes later – or perhaps it was years later? – no: neither is correct. It was quite definitely 16 seconds later. But now that I have remembered the time when, I find that I have forgotten the event which.

Chapter 460

Life is fraught with such difficulties. But a man is not necessarily right simply because he misunderstands modern physics. Let me content myself with a brief summary of this episode which merely remarks that as the sunlight was playing the trumpet or some such instrument among nearby houses, a sort of leaf was walking down the street mumbling to itself a few details of a lacerating well-remembered unfortunate conversation of a week ago. Is that sufficient for you?

Chapter 461

No, not a leaf. Of course it was not a leaf. Leaves do not do such things. It is other things which do such things. Ah yes; I remember now. The door opens and a badly bleeding life was thrown through. It was then shut again, as far as I recall. It complained about never having been born properly, and at once died. Ah well: whatever else you say about the universe – it does at least give us something to talk about.

Chapter 462

We all agreed that nothing much could be done about it now. After all: perhaps everyone is the wrong person. We went on talking about insignificant details among ourselves. Far off, in the distance (which is still not quite the same thing) someone is moving unseen away from us through the rooms.

Chapter 463

Perhaps Man invents future worlds to prevent him from understanding what this world really is. But in front of us, as we looked through the window, the past and the future continually changed places. We called this the present, and it hardly mattered to us which won the contest, provided that the same golden light stayed. If we lived for only one hour longer than we do, life would be eternal. Strange shy wandering minutes were intermittently picked out by that glorious light. It was something like a sunrise in the middle of the day. But if intelligence had really existed, what possible difference would it have made?

Chapter 464

Whether or not everybody is superior to everybody else, she was as wise as the inventor of rooms, and as wholly desirable as her face under any conditions – even the least obviously attractive, such as anger or sleeplessness. Perhaps it is astonishing how much Humanity has achieved, considering that well over 96% of them are so grossly incompetent. But inestimable virtues fell unnoticed from her brain as she walked. Other animals hope at most that the world is already a certain sort of place. Man hopes that it might be a different sort of place. Either may be right or wrong.

Chapter 465

Each of us is on some step or other of an infinite stairway, each supposing we are (if not at the very top) certainly on a natural landing, a cultured pause between flights. But it is all just stairs. Although we broke loose from the world with a jarring bump, I did not panic in the least, despite the fact that the room began to spin round, slowly at first, but with ever-increasing acceleration. More and more terrifying collisions began to occur.

Chapter 466

I knew that without taking risks of this nature nothing worthwhile would ever be achieved. True, I suspected that nothing very lasting would ever be achieved anyway. So I merely impregnated her and (towards that ordinary nightfall – what ordinary days great poetry is written on!) I drank a glass of milk which she had recently poured out of a cardboard carton, or something else not entirely dissimilar. I did not lie down on that particular floor in despair until much later in the year and slightly later in the century. Though it was at almost the same time in the history of the universe. Some say I will never rise again. Perhaps they are right. After all, true greatness in humans inheres in certain facial muscles of other humans.

Chapter 467

Tell me again, if you can, in which room has not at least one person realized that he (which is a sort of she) is or was dying? Perhaps long before the fact. Any room. Any office. This one too. And all the clocks, or most of them, continue to tick as nonchalantly as ever. We do not even look up.

Chapter 468

Not even though the chair is empty. And the country has perhaps been liberated.

The window is open. And yesterday's music has escaped. As has yesterday.

A fine moment for looking out in disbelief, sensing that the entire Universe is only a veneer. After all, there is veneer even in public executions. Yes – look! That world is still there!

But what of those staggering disproofs that I so recently read?

Chapter 469

This empty room too may be filled with a crowd which is not yet born. So I turn my head again, if this is a head. At times, one expects it would almost be worthwhile to blow up the earth, just in order to show the viruses (and perhaps the insects too – surely the lifeform spiritually nearest to the virus) who it is who is incontrovertibly in charge. But of course, the problem here is that they would be too stupid to notice. Indeed, they are so stupid they would probably survive.

Chapter 470

We can imagine everything, except reality. That's right: work away selflessly with your exquisite hands, if they really are hands. How can you be expected to suppose that all these movements are occurring well over 1500 years ago? An understatement, most probably, if anything. Everyone supposes that the universe is praising him personally or principally. Whereas, in fact, it is not even bored.

Chapter 471

After all, when did such a thing ever occur to *us*? But what care in the face! What loving expressions! What capacities! Does Time, too confident in its awareness that people live in a different world from the world they die in – whether either is the real world is highly doubtful – does it not have a grasp of at least the most basic requirements of decent manners? Will it not show a noble spirit even once, and mumble a simple straightforward apology for what it is doing? Is that too much to ask for?

Chapter 472

The door shuts. I trust she will return. I trust likewise that that was not a terminal illness which came in through the door, whether or not we are all here because one of our great-grandparents had a momentary sore knee. For what, in the end, will or can the precambrian era have been in its entirety but a woman's kimono lying on a kitchen chair for 1,500 million years?

Chapter 473

Ah, no. Still she is busily working at something which will not be finally rendered useless until another 37 years or seconds have passed. The intervals which we are wearing at the moment are not very expensive, perhaps – but they are so beautifully chosen! Years are a sort of guesswork anyway. All the same, I do rather hope that that was not the end of the Universe which came in through that door. Or is it the beginning? Or something similar? Or something in between? It can at times be difficult to make such subtle differences and distinctions out. I think you ought not to blame me for this failure, for though we may build an eight-lane highway for wisdom to enter a city by, it may sidle in (if at all) via the most obscure unmanned unnamed lane. Don't you think so?

Chapter 474

By the way, I should have mentioned before that I can see nothing here. Truly, astronomy is a form of flirting, but time opens the window then draws back, as horrified as usual at the sight of a single person passing by. Why is it so much easier to be an artist than to produce art? There are so many who, if only they did not write, we would so love to read them. But people continue talking instead, and nonsense supports nonsense.

Chapter 475

Know then, that time has passed and the sky has brightened. It is one of those ordinary and pointless afternoons when it occurs to oneself that, like any politician, one might in the end be little more than something which one's mother defecated.

Besides which, all reasonable dictionaries contain over a thousand words for each of which over a hundred thousand have killed or been killed. Obsolete dictionaries contain presumably more thousands. To God, there is an element of farce in mass-slaughter.

Chapter 476

A square of light moves slowly along the wall of the room. A single shelf of books contains a million lives. The sun shines on a flowery card, on a recently opened letter, on four or five great civilisations. Its rays stretch several zillion light years into space. A small notebook waits in the corner. Since something (let us call it the World) continues, how are we to say the last word on it? How is anyone ever to do so?

Chapter 477

So let me remark instead, even if it is little more than more or mere invention, that the first time he was told of such things the sun grew brighter from pure shame. Now there are those who say that it has got used to it. I have seen it shaking in the sky – I am not convinced. For, after all, no-one is wiser than food poisoning.

Chapter 478

Its chagrin, if you want my opinion, is that of a connoisseur who observes two larger than usual self-confident insects on the top of a picture-frame of a favoured image on the wall opposite him. They make their sexual intentions obvious, thereby causing the sun to dim a little, and awakening the usual asexual horror in the onlooker's heart. He picks up something – anything – the first thing to hand – perhaps an unreadable classic of modern or fairly modern literature, something like this – one which makes the best approximation which fiction can do to real life, which would be to get close enough to the target to be mistaken by the charitably-minded for a near-miss – and throws this (unless perhaps he prefers to use certain intimate moments left behind by a woman who is at present listening to a soi-disant expert on political economy in a white office-building of disheartening ugliness – albeit an appropriate one for the rulers of such a mediocre country, full of mental slaves and natural lackeys who are nonetheless forever congratulating themselves on their independence of mind – above which a meteorite is passing, unseen by any of the morose transients in the street below) – and throws this, I repeat, which is not wholly inappropriate for he would repeat the action if he could, at the insectual and probably incestuous copulation (though to flies we do not extend so strict a morality as we do to humans, who are in several ways different from insects), missing it by a moderate amount; and causing them to pause not a jot in their joyful exertions, even though as a result of them probably no great hero will shortly be born, who will lead his lethargic people to freedom, in what is in insect terms a comparatively short period of time, from out of this doleful depressing wet land. For nothing is so common as the other-wordly, and few enterprises are more difficult than the attempt to get in touch with someone of whom one knows only the name, address, fax and telephone-number.

Chapter 479

But even worse follows. The object penetrates the image, forcing an impressively vulvar rent in its fabric, out of which a steady stream of turbid water begins to flow or pour or leap but not spurt, causing confusion to the sole occupant of the room, who has been musing that Man invents fears, and then invents Gods to allay those fears. But even worse: this insecure incoherent invention itself gives rise to greater, unallayable fears.

Chapter 480

But even worse: it continues to penetrate the wall behind the image, entering the neighbouring room, surprising a girl who is rolling about in bed (presumably from a pure sense of fun – causing the sun to brighten considerably) – I should have mentioned before that the art-collector is dead by now of course – before it breaks out into the open air and now, continuing on in an inalienable trajectory which causes the sun to dim a little (or even to remain a little as it is), it passes for instance over an empty space of ground containing trees, clearly glimpsable through railings, where leaves or tears or years were falling in baffling profusion, beautiful and promising as a quietly talking woman standing with her back to someone who believes either that the worst griefs are those which lack a socially agreed name, or that a human being is rarely more innocently employed than when sexually assaulting a consenting tax-inspector. Or a little mirror bought in Arizona. Or kneeling.

Chapter 481

Now passing on without any of that casual cruelty which so often disfigures the sky, it ignored singing which floated up towards it (however pious); it ignored the sounds of doors opening and causing the sun neither to dim nor brighten, no matter how many eyes dilated at the sights thereby revealed; it ignored even the fact that while we sleep, everything laughs at us. Especially our voices. Do we return? The clock, standing in for eternity, keeps a straight face.

Chapter 482

Now, passing above a long white office-building of disheartening ugliness appropriate for those who pretended to their intimates that they were somehow the rulers of that country – many of the offices are at present empty (even though no-one in a position of power can quite believe that it is true throughout an entire waking day – is this me here? is power no more than this? where is the ultimate power, the real power? – in the next room perhaps?) and beyond into the petty-bourgeois, male-dominated, Eurocentric arachnoepterate depths of the superficial sky.

Chapter 483

Here, it ascended past stray wisps of cloud, fortunate exceptions to the general emptiness all round (for religion is a failure both of belief and of doubt), and continued, subject to its own less normal preference as regards gravitational attraction, upwards and ever upwards, although occasionally sideways, as empty as a window giving out onto a hectically busy street containing a pair of figures who had recently kissed in secret; as baffled as someone whose daughter or dearest hope (though not both) has just unsuspectedly died on a road not far from a curtained window behind which an empty bed struggles with historical importance; as surprised in a proud way as a skinny woman whose thighs a political giant of progressive tendencies has been talking deliriously of, to the exclusion of all else, as he died; as unimportant as death (which would be so far more impressive or convincing if only human beings did not fart as often as they do); as vital as superb old music no longer played; as terrifying as the fact that one can grow indifferent even to a woman whose vital charms one once devoured in genuine, impassioned kisses. Let no-one dare to claim that I have not given a full description of the phenomenon. It should be extremely easy to recognise now to whoever next sees it.

Chapter 484

Onwards for life it has continued, and now it has reached that area of sky through which doors pass – usually shut, although with an occasional slightly-opened one. Are we not all mirrors of each other? The sun is brighter than ever, or appears so and the meteorite (now in another century) begins to run into an irregular succession of solid cloudlets, which, despite their valorous attempts at preserving their required appearance of indifference, cannot wholly (and who would want them to?) disguise the fleeting smiles with which they now welcome the intrepid voyager on its return to its base. After all, the mere fact that no such being as God exists is surely no reason why we should not strive to fulfil his purposes. This is a very great mystery. (For so is utter nonsense frequently sanctified. Most wise utterances are simply wrong.)

Chapter 485

It would be crass arrogance on my part, which is to say I am very tired, to attempt to reduce the infinite complexity of the heavens to an elaborated arithmetical sequence. Let me merely point out that most of the little clouds were pleasantly unoccupied – whether permanently or temporarily I am unfortunately not allowed to say. This is none too great a defeat, as we

191

are formed in such a way as to make our bafflement inevitable. We should not read too much into this.

Chapter 486

But after a hundred or so empty ones had been passed, the meteorite ran alongside one which contained a cigarette packet still holding a single cigarette. What bizarre things one will find in the sky if one is only prepared to look for long enough! (This did not tempt it for, like all meteorites, it does not smoke tobacco. But I would suggest that the reason why Humanity thinks of the sea as being angry may well be because it has accidentally dropped so much money into it in the course of numerous, pointless journeys. If this is too deep for you, accept merely the supposition that life can be beautiful and life can also be ugly. This truth is too complicated for many.)

Chapter 487

Two objects further on, it passed a cloud which held another, equally small box. This contained half the treasures of human civilization. Because we are capable of infinite stupidities, we suspect we are immortal. But here a tiny divine figure, partly dressed and in white, was trying to stuff it (What? If you have forgotten, call it merely the universe – for the universe does not kill us) into one of the apertures of her body, in a spirit (as it seemed) of pure fun. This, by the way, was God. Try and describe a more credible one, if you wish. I can predict with some confidence that you will utterly fail. Granted, one of the advantages of being old is that one is old. However, this is frequently also one of the advantages of being young. What does it matter?

Chapter 488

The next 103 stations all contained different varieties of morning light, each equally suitable for a promising day appearing over a neighbouring line of rooftops of considerable architectural interest, while nearby someone lies sleeping, of overwhelming architectural interest.

Chapter 489

Perhaps this may also be the source of small unintentional unignorable sounds which are being emitted with a scarcely endurable lack of appreciation of their vast universal significance. Let us hear no more of spectacular radio sources! (An odd thing to say, given that I do not think I have mentioned them here before.) For what could happiness be but a particular comport of the brain? It is as if the divine spark of the organism has at last found a bra that fits it. I hope I do not seem obsessed. Or rather: I hope that such is not the reality.

Chapter 490

However – onward sped the meteorite or object of whichever description, implacable as the randomness or order of randomness which dictates the creation of an endearingly beautiful vagina among humans; riffling happily through the frills of time, that impossible substance or decoration thanks to which there are now or now appear to be such enchanting holes in the sky and its local environment.

Chapter 491

Well, aren't there?

Chapter 492

Well? Aren't there?

Chapter 493

Eh? What do you think – yes, *you*.

Chapter 494

Can you not give up even one or two of your less endearing habits and try to answer – or at least confront – these overwhelming and fascinating questions? None of them?

Chapter 495

After all, if carbon cannot achieve greatness, then what can?

Chapter 496

Since the Universe is not a question, what answer should we give?

Chapter 497

If life lasted forever, it would still be unbelievable, would it not?

Chapter 498

Surely the truly wise man tries to live his life as if he had just died a few seconds ago? What do you think? Or a few thousand million years ago?

Chapter 499

You would not deny that certainty is almost certainly the opposite of wisdom, I hope.

Chapter 500

Well: would you?